2024

# BOOKS OF HORROR INDIE BRAWL

# ANTHOLOGY

# CONTENDER LIST

Puzzle House by Duncan Ralston
Gone To See The Riverman by Kristopher Triana
Bunker Dogs by Gage Greenwood
Beta by Sammy Scott
Inside The Devil's Nest by John Durgin
I Found Puppets Living in my Apartment Walls
    by Ben Farthing
In The Tall Trees by Angel Van Atta
Left To You by Daniel J Volpe
Hollow by Mike Salt
By The Light of Dead Stars by Andrew Van Wey
Lovely, Dark and Deep by Megan Stockton
These Things Linger by Dan Franklin
Cadaverous by Jay Bower
Cursed by Leigh Kenny
A Dark and Rising Tide by Debra Castaneda
Through The Eyes of Desperation: Red Version
    by Aron Beauregard
The Boyfriend by DE McCluskey
Jones 1963 by Devin Cabrera
Soul Searcher by Justin Boote
Echoes of Home by M L Rayner
This is Where We Talk Things Out by Caitlin Marceau
The Odds by Jeff Strand
How Much To? By Matt Shaw
Stuck by Ben Young
Tent Revival by Edmund Stone
Beast of Burden by Judith Sonnet
Slashtag by Jon Cohn
Gollitok by Andrew Najberg
Devil's Creek by Todd Keisling
Blender Babies by Jon Athan
Daughter's Drawings by Nick Botic
Mine by LM Kaplin

# CHECKLIST

2024
BOOKS OF HORROR
INDIE BRAWL

BEAST OF BURDEN
JUDITH SONNET

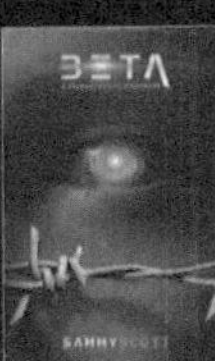

BETA

BLENDER BABIES
JON ATHAN

THE BOYFRIEND
D E McCLUSKEY

2024
BOOKS OF HORROR
INDIE BRAWL

BUNKER DOGS
GAGE GREENWOOD

BY THE LIGHT OF DEAD STARS
ANDREW VAN WEY

JAY BOWER
CADAVEROUS

CURSED
LEAH KENNY

A Dark and Rising Tide
Debra Castaneda

DAUGHTER'S DRAWINGS
NICK ROTIC

DEVIL'S CREEK
TODD KEISLING

M. L. RAYNER
ECHOES OF HOME

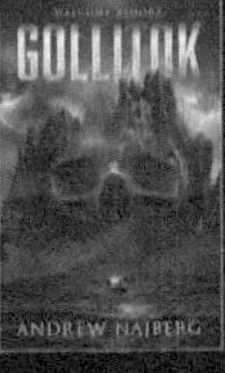

GOLLITOK
ANDREW NAJBERG

GONE TO SEE THE RIVER MAN
KRISTOPHER TRIANA

HOLLOW
MIKE SALT

HOW MUCH TO..?

I FOUND PUPPETS LIVING IN MY APARTMENT WALLS
BEN FARTHING

in the tall trees

INSIDE THE DEVIL'S NEST
JOHN DURGIN

DEVIN CABRERA
JONES 1963

LEFT TO YOU
DANIEL J. VOLPE

LOVELY, DARK & DEEP
MEGAN STOCKTON

MINE.
LOU KAPLIN

JEFF STRAND
THE ODDS

PUZZLE HOUSE
DUNCAN RALSTON

SLASHTAG
JON COHN

SEARCHERS
JUSTIN BOOTE

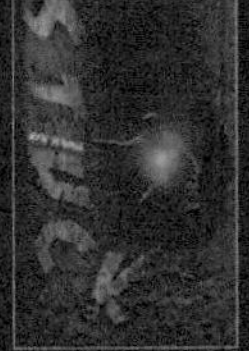

2024
BOOKS OF HORROR
INDIE BRAWL

TENT REVIVAL
EDMUND STONE

THESE THINGS LINGER
DAN FRANKLIN

THIS IS WHERE WE TALK THINGS OUT

THROUGH THE EYES OF DESPERATION
THE RED VERSION
ARON BEAUREGARD

2024
BOOKS OF HORROR
INDIE BRAWL

ELIMINATION BRACKET
1: PUZZLE HOUSE
32: BLENDER BABIES
16: EYES OF DESPERATION: RED
17: JONES 1963
9: HOLLOW
24: STUCK
8: LEFT TO YOU
25: TENT REVIVAL
4: BETA
29: DEVIL'S CREEK
13: THESE THINGS LINGER
20: SOUL SEARCHERS
12 CADAVEROUS
21: THIS IS WHERE WE TALK THINGS OUT
5: INSIDE THE DEVIL'S NEST
28: GOLLITOK
1: GONE TO SEE THE RIVER MAN
31: MINE
15: A DARK AND RISING TIDE
10: THE BOYFRIEND
10: BY THE LIGHT OF DEAD STARS
23: HOW MUCH TO?
7: IN THE TALL TREES
23: BEAST OF BURDEN
3: BUNKER DOGS
30: DAUGHTER'S DRAWINGS
14: CURSED
19: ECHOES OF HOME
11: LOVELY, DARK AND DEEP
22: THE ODDS
6: I FOUND PUPPETS...
27: SLASHTAG

This book is dedicated to the admins and moderators of Books of Horror. They have created a unique and special place for readers and authors to come together and share their love of horror books.

Hans Curtis
Tiffany Koplin
RJ Roles
Erin Wilczynski
Heather Ann Larson


Join Books of Horror on Facebook today to be part of this amazing community and take part in future brawl voting and other fun events.

# TABLE OF CONTENDERS

# LEADERBOARD

# INTRODUCTION

## SEAN MCDONOUGH

The cruelty of these authors.

To beat me out for a slot in the 2024 Indie Brawl, and then to turn around and ask me to write the introduction to their short story anthology. As if they'd just cut my legs off and asked me to join them for an evening stroll.

The sadism. The sheer, unadulterated evil that must beat in their black hearts. Is it any wonder that they wrote such magnificently horrific novels? That they could conjure such masterpieces of wickedness?

...And then, worst of all, to actually get to interact with them! To see, firsthand, the joy they take in their work and to witness how they support each other and appreciate their readers!

What a bunch of monsters.

The Indie Brawl began in 2023 as an offshoot of the Horror March Madness tournament I'd done for a couple years. Some of the voters asked about letting indie and group authors participate, but I was leery. I didn't want it to turn into a popularity contest where everyone voted for their friends. I wanted it to be about the books, not the authors.

But thanks to some prodding and input from Mistress Tiffany (man, she can wear you down), we worked out a nomination process and, most important of all, an extended reading period to help level the playing field.

As it turned out, I was half right. The Indie Brawl didn't become a popularity contest, but it did turn out to be a popularity celebration. What we witnessed in the 2023 Indie Brawl was a massive outpouring of enthusiasm for everything we adore about horror as writers and readers. Slashers, ghosts, psychological. So many different forms of horror fiction were on display, and each one had its own legion of supporters shouting its praises. It's a cliché to say, but there were no losers.

And there are no losers this time, either. The celebration has only gotten bigger. More entrants fighting for a spot. More bookstores putting up Indie Brawl displays. More readers coming into the tent to see what all the fuss is about.

And more celebrations of horror like the book you hold in your hands. Justin Boote floated the idea out for an anthology, and Broken Brain Books and the authors here reached out and grabbed it with both hands. It's another opportunity for these immensely talented authors to play with the worlds and characters they love and one more chance for the readers to remember just why they love this butchershop of a genre so much.

Ding, ding, fight fans. Don't be afraid to get up close.

# A Hole in The Switch

## Gage Greenwood

Doctors' waiting rooms always looked so drab and un-inviting, at least from what Roth remembered of them. It was a long time since he last sat in one, but if Dr. Renard's waiting room was any indication, psychiatrists followed the pattern of wanting their patients to experience deep depression before entering the office.

He couldn't complain, though. Not many doctors were willing to see their patients long after hours, especially at eleven o'clock at night. Of course, the time of the appointment proved the least unusual aspect of this visit. First, Renard booked him, not the other way around. She waltzed right up to him at Cuddy's and said, "You're lonely, and your life is repetitive. You're ready to snap from the cyclic and boring lifestyle." She slid a card across the bar, unconcerned that a beer glass ringlet wet the edges. "Call my receptionist and book an appointment." Then she did something no one had done to Roth in many years. She touched him, putting her hand on top of his. "I specialize in the strange."

With a playful wink, she stepped backward and walked away before Roth could gather enough wits to respond. He searched for her later in the bar among the sea of drunks but couldn't find her. It was as if she came there solely to drop that card in front of him while he sipped his Sam Adams. And maybe she had. "I specialize in the strange," she had said.

*She couldn't have meant... But obviously, she did.*

Probably a good thing she gave him no time to speak, because as a reflex, he probably would have told her to fuck off. In fact, he spent the entire night boiling from the encounter. How dare she? She didn't know him. He had a good life, better than most! The "I specialize in the strange" stuck out to him, and he knew he would have to dig into that, but all the shrink talk about his feelings was a swing and a miss.

But the next night, he found himself drawn back to the conversation repeatedly. No matter what he did, her words cut into his brain like razor blades. Maybe she knew him better than he knew himself, because if she hadn't said it, he never would have recognized just how fucking miserable he was.

So, four days later, he sat in her office, scoffing at the beige walls and sickly yellow lighting. A receptionist sat at her desk clicking away at a keyboard. A receptionist! At 11:00 p.m.! What kind of doctor's office was this?

Each minute he waited for his session, he doubted coming here. What value could he possibly gain from it? He certainly couldn't be honest unless the doctor *really* meant she specialized in the strange, which he doubted.

The office doors swung open, and Dr. Renard smiled at Roth. "Ready?"

He rolled his tongue over his top teeth and said, "Yup."

He stopped short of entering when he saw a teenage girl sitting on a couch in the office. He had never seen a head doctor before, but he had watched enough movies to know how the sessions went. As far as he knew, there wasn't supposed to be a third party with the patient and doctor.

Dr. Renard put her hand on the small of his back. Another unexpected touch. It sent shivers up his body. "Don't worry. It'll all make sense soon. I promise."

He stepped in and moved out of the doctor's way but otherwise stood in place, waiting for directions on where to sit. He would have guessed the couch, but someone else sat there. In movies, the patient always lay down, crossed their arms, and stared at the ceiling. He couldn't do that with some teenage girl sitting in his spot.

Dr. Renard waved her hand toward the other side of the couch. "Have a seat."

So, he wouldn't get to lay down like in the movies. He found this disappointing.

He sat next to the girl. They shot each other a quick glance and an awkward smile before returning their attention to Dr. Renard, who sat across from them.

Roth had an atypical sense of smell. It wasn't just that it was strong but that it was *smart*. He could isolate and separate different odors, pushing aside the most noticeable ones to sniff out the hidden. The girl sitting next to him wore Love Spell perfume from Victoria's Secret. But Roth focused on her mouth, where the scent of chokecherries reigned supreme. He knew a man who lost four horses in one night thanks to a chokecherry shrub. Supposedly they weren't deadly for humans, and people even put them in their jams, but Roth had never smelled them so prominently, as if the girl sat at a chokecherry tree and plucked it bare.

Dr. Renard crossed her legs. "Roth, thank you for coming in. I do things a little differently than other psychiatrists as you can probably guess from your near midnight appointment. It'll seem strange at first, but I promise you'll find it worth it in the end, because the other thing I am, outside of unorthodox, is effective."

He had a lot to unpack from her introduction. First, she thanked *him* for coming in, reaffirming that she planned his appointment, not him seeking professional help. And then the woman who told him she specialized in the strange, presumably *knowing* what that meant to Roth, said *he* would find things strange in the appointment. If she worried that an oddity like Roth would find the session peculiar, he had to admit, it piqued his curiosity.

She continued. "While this isn't a group session, per say, it will be a session between the both of you. Molly will go first, and you'll host the second half of the hour. I know you may not feel comfortable sharing with another patient present, but I promise, by the time Molly's half hour is up, you'll feel better about it." She gave him a large faux smile. "For now, all you need to do is relax and give Molly your attention."

The idea of listening to a teenage girl whine about

her high school woes made him want to punch himself in the skull, but he would play along. This whole visit was an exercise in playing along. Curiosity killed the cat, but Roth had lived through enough lifetimes that he sometimes thought curiosity was the only thing keeping him alive.

No longer focusing on him, Dr. Renard said, "So, Molly, you've mentioned having bad dreams again."

*Dreams. Jesus Christ, this was going to be a long hour.*

Molly slipped her flip flops off and put her feet on the couch as she crossed her legs. She looked like a Buddha statue minus the wisdom. And she dressed like an idiot. Florescents. It reminded Roth of late 80s, early 90s cornball hip-hop videos. She had a neon green muscle shirt that gave away her white bra on the sides, blindingly bright pink spandex-style shorts, and a rainbow of colors dyed into her long otherwise-blonde hair. He knew her hair was blonde because the dye job was too shoddy to cover the roots or ends.

He presumed her *dreams* would be as vapid as her appearance. At least he would learn who the newest heartthrobs were. NSYNC? Were they still popular? Or did they fall out with the last century? How long ago was Y2K? Roth couldn't remember. Three years, he guessed.

Molly tucked her hair behind her ears and smiled. "Yeah, the dreams are getting more intense, so I had to investigate."

Dr. Renard's forehead scrunched, and she scooted forward in her seat. "What do you mean you investigated? You know you're not supposed to do that kind of thing without guidance."

"I know, but it was calling me."

Dr. Renard shook her hands violently. "Exactly. And what if the thing calling you was bad?"

Roth leaned back, taking this all in. Maybe he misjudged the situation. Was Molly... like him?

Molly crossed her arms across her chest like a grumpy child. "I knew it wasn't."

Dr. Renard gave her scolding eyes. "Tell me about the dream and where it led you."

"Ever since I left the island and moved to Tanner's Switch, I've been hearing a heartbeat. Sometimes it's soft, and sometimes it's really loud. At first, I thought it was different based on the time of day, but then I realized it was all about location. As soon as I determined that, I tried traveling to it."

"Physically traveling to it or mentally? Not that I approve of either."

"Mentally. At first. But every time I got so close I could *feel* the heartbeat as if it were in my own chest, it would soften and I'd be back to square one. I decided I was wrong, that it wasn't a location thing, and I went back to studying the times. Maybe it happened at noon one day, midnight the next, and five on Friday, but I guess there could have been a pattern."

*What the fuck were these people talking about?*

"Was there?" Dr. Renard asked.

Molly shook her head. "No. But I was right when I thought the heartbeat had a location. I just didn't realize it was moving. One day, it just clicked in my mind, and that's when I knew I needed to physically go to the beat."

"What did you find?"

"I found a hole in Tanner's Switch. It's always moving, but it's always around. I found the heartbeat in a parking lot by the boat launch on 91. When I stepped on the center of the dirt lot, my foot went through the earth as if the ground were made of paper."

Roth stepped in now, utterly confused. "In the middle of a parking lot? Wouldn't other people have fallen into it?"

Dr. Renard lifted a finger, telling him to shush. "I don't think the hole she's speaking of is the kind of thing that affects normal people." She moved her eyes back to Molly. "Where did it lead? Were you able to see or did you just get the hell out of there?"

Molly smiled. "Oh, I dove right in." This admission led to a giggle.

"What did you find?" Roth asked, somehow invested in something he wholly didn't understand.

Did her eyes turn red? He couldn't tell.

"I saw Tanner's Switch."

Dr. Renard tilted her head. "What do you mean?"

Molly sat up. "I saw Tanner's Switch on fire, and people screaming into cameras. I saw dead birds and lampposts. I saw mist. I saw people moving around and living their lives with no idea what's to come, what's about to happen to all of us. And it terrified me, seeing the faces who don't know. It was a mistake to jump in." Her eyes filled with water. "Because now I have the burden of carrying this secret forever." She turned her head to Roth, and back to Dr. Renard. "Because none of you can ever know the truth. You'd snap."

Dr. Renard stood up and slashed her arm across the room like she was karate chopping imaginary wood. "That's enough. You can *never* speak about this to anyone. Not even a hint at the heartbeat. Okay? Not even to me. And I'll probably try to get answers from you in moments of weakness, but you can never, ever tell me anything about it."

Molly nodded.

Roth eyed them both, unable to hide how ridiculous he found them both. "Is this some kind of skit? What the fuck are you all going on about?"

Dr. Renard slid her hand down her skirt as she sat down, fully back to normal. "Your turn, Roth."

He laughed. "I thought you said I would change my mind after her time was up. All I saw was ten minutes of jibber-jabber. Nonsense."

"Yes, Molly's meeting today was not what I expected. It's normally a little showier. I'll demonstrate. See, you probably think her talking about weird dreams is no big deal, but Molly's dreams are not like ours. She hasn't slept in over a decade."

Roth laughed again.

"Molly, show him how you sleep."

She slowly turned her head to him. Yes, her eyes were indeed red. Her neck snapped back and her whole body left the couch. It shot up to the ceiling like a bullet and smashed hard into the stucco. The whole room shook. Meanwhile, Molly's body slid from one side of the room to the other before dropping back to the floor. Breeze escaped her like her skin was a fan, blowing cool air on Roth.

And then she was up, completely back to normal. She giggled. "Cool, huh?"

Dr. Renard said, "Convinced? Do you want to send her a message in the black mist?"

Roth said, "Huh?"

"Don't play coy. How many people have you killed, Roth?"

He blinked, a nervous tic. "What?"

Her eyebrows went up. "Ever kill a demon?"

He laughed. "You have the wrong guy."

Dr. Renard pointed to Molly. "She's not like you, but she can still read your black mist. Send it to her."

"No."

"NOW!" She slammed her fist on the table.

He opened his mouth, and a cloud of black steam twirled out of him. It floated across the room, and Molly swallowed it.

She licked her lips. "Oh, he's a bad one." Her nose scrunched cutely. "It tastes good. He's mean to the ones he's killed. It's not just for the need. He gets his fill and then toys with them."

"Fuck you," Roth said and jumped across the table, teeth out, ready to rip into the doctor, his curiosity not thick enough to coat his rage. Halfway between the couch and the doctor's chair, his body froze in midair. He couldn't move, not even to open or close his eyes.

Molly walked in front of him and placed a finger on his forehead. "He's never tasted a demon, so he's pretty weak. I mean, he finished off a human yesterday, so he's normal strong, but he's only ever eaten people. Nothing that could make him super strong."

"What's his name?"

"Roth Fischer."

"No, I mean check the files and see what his name will be in the bunker."

"Oh!" Molly skipped to a file cabinet in the corner and flipped through some manilla folders. She took the folder over to Roth and slapped it on his forehead. "You, mister, will now be William Henry Harrison."

For the first time in over a century, Roth's heart raced. The one thing in his body that moved. In a way, he was thankful. It felt good to feel something again.

Renard hit a button, and the receptionist walked in.

"Take him to the tunnels. Molly has him frozen. He won't be moving for a long time."

The receptionist did as she was told.

# Beneath The Devil's Nest

## John Durgin

Andy Hixon parked outside the gate, reading the worn sign with its chipped, blue paint—Welcome to Bird's Nest. Except Bird's was crossed out, defaced by the word "Devil's." He shook his head, hoping his employee, Ryan Wise, aka "the Wise man," didn't see the nickname before he drove through the open gate. He looked over at Ryan and was relieved to see him still scrolling aimlessly through his phone.

Andy drove through the opening and down a steep driveway as a large house came into view, its appearance a reminder that disaster had struck recently. The porch had collapsed, leaving a pile of debris sprawled across the driveway. But they weren't here for the home, they were here for the pond.

Andy passed the house and continued down a dirt path until he came to the end of the road, then carefully turned the truck around. He kept his eyes locked on the review mirror as he backed the Hydrovac truck toward the tree line that led to the green pond. In the passenger seat, Ryan continued to scroll through his cellphone. He swiped left and right on some dating app, randomly letting out a snort when a girl decided to show too much skin. Andy couldn't help feeling like he was supervising a middle-grade tool bag half the time.

"How long we thinking this job will take?" Ryan asked, still mindlessly swiping his phone.

Andy looked over at him, noticing his Batman bobblehead jittering around on the dashboard with every pothole they backed over. Behind the bobblehead, a picture of his wife and two kids stared back at him, their beautiful smiles warming his heart.

"About six, seven hours, I s'pose. We need to drain it all the way down to the fucking mire. The lady said she wants to make sure there's no more water in that pond by the time we leave."

"Why you think they hired us from out of state for such a pissant job? Seems they coulda saved a ton of money to hire someone close by," Ryan said.

"Fuck if I know. But I'm not about to turn down fifteen grand to do a quick job like this. Jerry should already be here with the sub pump. We'll get it set up, then we'll head out of here for lunch. Guy at the gas station said Plaza Pizza over in Newport is the place to go around here. Then we'll come back and clean up."

Andy parked the truck at the edge of the trail, unable to get too close to the water due to the number of trees blocking the pond. But they came prepared for roadblocks. After giving an estimate much higher than a job this size would normally cost, Andy expected the customer to balk at the price and move on. It was what he always did with jobs he didn't want. When she accepted without hesitation, he got his crew together and pushed back the jobs already scheduled ahead of it.

They climbed out of the truck and got to work, connecting the hose to the tank, then leading it down toward the water. Andy's other employee, Jerry, had already parked his pickup truck at the edge of the tree line and carried the sub pump over to the dock. The hardest part of the job would be getting the pump into the deepest part of the water, but they brought rope to help guide it down. Luckily, the dock went far enough out that it reached close to the center of the pond.

"About time you pecker heads showed up. I've been sitting here the last half hour breathing in this dead fish smell. If I wanted to inhale that, I'd spend another night with Andy's mom," Jerry sniggered.

"Hey, fuck off. I told you what time to get to the job site. Not my fault you can't tell time without your Mickey Mouse watch," Andy said.

Ryan shook his head and laughed as he hooked the naked end of the hose to the pump.

"If Andy's mom really smells like this, why the hell would you spend the night with her in the first place, you sick fuck?" Ryan asked Jerry.

"Sometimes easy's better than pretty..."

Andy gave Jerry a shove, causing his employee to almost fall off the dock into the murky water. Jerry grabbed hold of the support beam connected to the railing and caught his balance as Ryan and Andy busted out laughing.

"Real fucking funny! Didn't you guys hear about what happened here? Why they want us draining this place? I'd prefer not to go swimming with that fucking lore spreading around town."

Andy looked nervously at Ryan. Of course Andy knew—he was the boss. He did his research before agreeing to any job. But he continued to play it off with Ryan like he had no idea because Ryan believed in all that voodoo ghost shit. Andy chalked it up to a crazy family man going on a killing spree, not some supernatural cult living beneath the water.

"What's he talking about, Andy? You said you didn't know why they hired us," Ryan said.

"Wise man, just do your damn job. If I turned down every offer that had a shady past, I'd be out of business."

Ryan shook his head and continued the set up. Andy scanned the water, curious why the green had a slight glow to it, almost like pea soup mixed with antifreeze. He couldn't see more than a few inches beneath the surface, which made him a bit nervous to lower the pump to the pond floor. If there were any rocks or uneven terrain down there, it could damage the equipment. Still, he was being paid enough that he didn't have to worry about minor damage.

After everything was set up, Andy did one last pass on all the equipment to make sure it was connected securely, then he and Ryan lowered the sub pump to the bottom of the pond using the pully rope. When they felt it reach the bottom, Andy wiped the sweat from his brow and turned to head back to the shore. He froze mid-step when he spotted Jerry standing rigid in the center of the dock, facing the water. Andy couldn't see his face, but he noticed Jerry's fingers were curled into his palms, digging at the skin.

"Jer? Ya good, man?"

Jerry didn't acknowledge him, continuing to stare straight out at the water. Ryan came up and stood next to Andy to see what was wrong. He swore under his breath and sped past Andy, grabbing Jerry by the shoulder and turning him. Andy almost screamed. Jerry's eyes were rolling in the back of his head, only the whites showing as he whispered something to himself.

"What the fuck man, cut the shit!" Ryan snapped, shaking Jerry.

Andy hoped Jerry was messing with Ryan, but either way, it made the hair on the back of his neck stand on end. Jerry blinked, and his eyes went back to normal as his posture relaxed.

"What the hell..." he mumbled.

"You two need to tell me what the fuck's going on right now! If this is some attempt to get in my head, congrad-u-fucking-lations, it worked," Ryan said.

"I don't know what just happened, man. Stop shouting... My damn head hurts now. What was I doing?" Jerry asked.

Andy and Ryan exchanged worried glances, unsure what to say.

"You didn't smoke some of Satan's lettuce while you waited for us to get here, did you?" Andy asked.

"You're an asshole, you know that? Of course I didn't," Jerry said, then pushed past Andy and exited the dock.

Andy sighed and looked up to the overcast sky.

"Sorry, man. Just trying to figure out what the hell's happening. Let's start the sub pump before the storm comes and go get some grub. We'll come back in a few hours, and this should be moving right along. Hope you don't mind us squeezing in your truck since we need to leave the Hydrovac here while the pump goes," Andy said.

"As long as you sit in the middle and go skiing," Jerry muttered.

They all laughed and packed into the truck, leaving the pond behind.

A few hours later, they pulled back into the job site, with full bellies and a nice afternoon buzz. They hadn't planned on drinking as much as they did, but Andy wanted to celebrate after landing such a top-paying job. The pizza was top-notch as advertised. While they ate their lunch, they started up a conversation with a man there by himself who said he grew up in the area and was home to visit his ailing mother. Howie Burke was his name, a nice guy—until Andy told him why they were in town. Howie insisted they should forget about the job and leave, that it wasn't safe to be down by the pond. As if Ryan needed another reason to be freaked out, when Howie told them they should leave the place immediately, Ryan was ready to skip town. But they calmed him down and went back to their pizza and beer.

"Let's go see how much progress we made while we were gone," Jerry said. His sentence was met with a crack of thunder, reminding them a severe storm was closing in. Light sprinkles had begun to fall—a warning before what was likely to be a torrential downpour.

The three of them hopped out of the truck and followed the trail through the tall grass down to the dock. Andy was elated to see the water had already almost completely drained. Enough so they could walk out to the middle of the pond and only be ankle deep. The three of them trudged through the thick gunk as their rubber boots stuck to the ground like a suction cup, making squishy fart sounds with each step.

"Hey Andy, is this what your mom sounds like when Jerry's pounding her?" Ryan asked.

"Funny, asshole. Be careful or the pond monsters will get ya," Andy said, no longer concerned with scaring his employee. It brought him great joy to see the smile on Ryan's face turn to a frown.

"Hey, what the hell's that over there near the center of the pond?" Jerry asked.

"I'm not falling for it. You assholes can try and scare me all you want," Ryan said.

"No, I'm serious. It dips in the middle like there's a drain sucking some of the water down."

Andy scratched his head in confusion. Jerry was right. He had ignored the fact the pond drained much faster than it should have and that the tank on the truck would have been nearly full if it had, in fact, sucked this much water up. It was too good to be true. But now they had an answer as to why. It just didn't add up.

"This makes no fucking sense... If there was a drain in the center, man-made or not, the water should've never been this full to begin with," Andy said.

They approached the center of the pond, the water still ankle deep and the color of a blended avocado. Andy knelt at the dip, feeling beneath the surface for the culprit. All he felt was an empty space, like there was a void below that led to complete nothingness. Jerry stepped around him, getting too close to the spot for Andy's liking.

"Be careful, Jerry. Might be a sink—"

Jerry dropped beneath the surface, disappearing completely like he had fallen in the deep end of a pool instead of six inches of pond water. There was a brief scream before he vanished with water swirling around his body like a flushed toilet.

"Jer!" Ryan yelled, charging toward the now-empty space.

Andy's heart obliterated his chest muscles, but he remained focused enough to put a hand up to stop Ryan's advance.

"Wait! It's not safe. We can't help him if we fall down there with him. We need to wait for the rest of the water to drain so we can see what we're dealing with."

"He's gonna fucking drown, man! We need to do something *now*!"

Andy felt himself beginning to panic, unsure of what to do. He couldn't exactly go under and try to find Jerry, not when the water was as thick as stew. They both stood over the spot, neither making a move. And then Jerry's head shot above the surface, his eyes wide with terror.

"Elllp me!" He gargled out, then went back under.

*Was that blood on his face?* Andy thought.

When Jerry sank below again, the water went with

him, draining into the open space. A small puddle re-mained, bubbling until it also vanished, leaving only a long, zigzagging split in the ground.

"Jerry!" Andy shouted.

Andy and Ryan dropped to their knees next to the sub pump, looking into the hole. The crack had to be at least ten feet long, starting narrow on each end then getting wider as it got closer to the center.

*Just wide enough for a body to fall through.*

"I can't see shit down there. You got your phone?" Andy asked.

"Fuck, I left it in the truck. I can run and grab it," Ryan said.

It was company policy (Andy's policy) to leave phones in the work trucks, not just to prevent them from falling in water but to make sure employees did their damn job without distractions. Andy regretted that rule as he continued to look through the crack, mindful not to get too close.

Something shifted a few feet below in the darkness.

Before Andy could get a second look, Ryan shouted behind him.

"Oh shit! Andy? You need to see this..."

Andy turned to see what had Ryan worked up, and his mouth dropped in awe. Scattered bones and skeletons poked up out of the muck, decorating the pond floor. There was no possible way they were there before or the guys would have felt them crunch beneath their feet as they walked to the pump.

"What the hell..." he whispered.

He scanned the graveyard of the cult, or the cult's vic-tims, losing count of how many bodies were dispersed around.

The sound of something digging beneath the ground brought Andy's attention back to the hole just as a hand shot out of the crack, grabbing hold of his ankle.

"Help me out! Heeelp!" Jerry yelled.

Andy shouted an unnatural cry and looked down to see Jerry's face peering up from the hole, his eyes full of terror.

"They're coming back!"

Without hesitation, Andy reached down and grabbed hold of his hand, almost losing his grip as the algae and sludge lathered Jerry's skin. There was more movement behind Jerry. Multiple sets of white eyes dotted the inky black space behind his friend.

"Jerry! Watch out!"

They pulled on Jerry, ripping his hand back into the hole, breaking free of Andy's grasp. Whispers buzzed beneath the ground, but Andy couldn't hear what they were saying. Jerry screamed over them as the figures surrounded him, suffocated him, ripped him apart. A green hand covered in worms and algae wrapped around Jerry's face, one of its long fingers sticking into his mouth and pulling. Andy heard the tear of Jerry's cheek being ripped apart as his employee continued to bellow in agony. The figures swarmed him like a horde of angry wasps. Andy had a fleeting thought that was *just* what these things were—angry wasps whose nest was disturbed. And they were vicious.

Jerry's cries cut off, then his body disappeared into the darkness. Andy remained crouched, too shocked to do anything else. But then he realized the figures behind Jerry had stopped moving or making noise. He brought his attention back to the hole to find all of them staring directly at him, their hazy orbs burning into his soul.

"Oh fuck..."

He slowly backed up, keeping his eyes glued to the opening as the rain picked up intensity. Had he been paying attention to where he was going, he would have seen the large femur bone of a past victim behind him. Instead, he tripped over it and fell to his ass, landing hard in the muck. The crack in the ground began to branch out, weaving toward him as if it was hot on his trail. A dozen or more hands dug through the sludge, forcing their way above ground like a flower after a rainstorm. Only instead of beautiful flower petals, Andy saw jagged, caked fingernails clawing at the ground to gain traction. He tried to get up and run, wondering where in the hell Ryan was and why he wasn't back yet to help. One of the hands came up behind him, grabbing hold of his wrist. The nails dug into his skin, drawing blood, and continued to squeeze until his wrist bone snapped. Andy fell to his back, unable to hold himself up.

Another crack of thunder launched his heart into his throat as the pain pulsated through his broken wrist. He tried to break free, but the hand holding him had an inhuman strength, refusing to let go. Instead, it continued squeezing, pulling Andy toward the newly formed section of the crack in the ground. Rain splashed off his face as he tried to break free. Then his hand was pulled into the hole, disappearing below. Andy dropped face down, unable to stand his ground.

A white eye peered up at him through the crack.

*"Join us... Be one with Vodyanoy..."*

Suddenly, the fear that had consumed Andy a moment

ago was replaced by a devout calmness. That voice—it got into his head. He wanted to join them. The white eye remained locked on him, and he found himself transfixed by its gaze.

"Ok..." he said numbly.

Ryan came running across the empty pond, losing one of his boots along the way through the sludge.

"Andy! Boss! You ok? I got my phone..."

Andy stood up from the ground, his broken wrist leaving his hand dangling limply. Ryan noticed it and ran to his boss.

"What the fuck happened?"

"I'm fine," Andy said blankly.

"Fine? Your goddamn hand is falling off! I'm calling 9-1-1!"

Ryan lifted his phone to dial, and Andy struck him in the face, dropping his unsuspecting employee to the ground. Andy stood over him, set on making sure the phone never got used again.

"There's no need to call anyone..."

"Boss, what the fuck? Have you lost your damn mind? Jerry's stuck down there. We need to get help!"

"Jerry's with us now. And so are you," Andy said, his mouth forming a sinister smile.

Ryan squinted in confusion as multiple hands rose from the muck around him, grabbing hold of his limbs. He looked down and screamed, but he was unable to break free of their strength. The hands were moon white with green veins branching across their skin. They squeezed Ryan, holding him in a crucifix position.

"Andy! Help me! What the fuck!"

The hands pulled him lower, his body beginning to

submerge into the muddy ground. The crack beneath him widened, allowing his body to be swallowed by the nest. He screamed, but his mouth sank below and filled with the swampy substance. His eyes bulged, begging Andy to help one last time. Instead, Andy smiled again, then lowered himself to the ground as well. He allowed the nest to take him, to make him one with Vodyanoy. He could no longer see Ryan, but he didn't care. He stared up at the gray sky, allowing the rain to pelt off his face as he sank lower and lower to be with his new family. It was time for Vodyanoy to return.

**THE END**

# A Mother's Choice

## Angel Van Atta

Betty was sleeping soundly when it happened, when her world went from normal and easy to a sudden hellish nightmare she never imagined. At least, not while awake.

Her dreams were silly things that night, filled with silly people, and a perfect little smile played on her lips as she lay there, eyes closed to the world and what was coming. It was perhaps the very last smile she would ever make. The very last smile, and she wasn't even awake to know it was there.

Her eyes came open when she heard the people screaming from next door, or perhaps from a door farther down. It was hard to say exactly where they were coming from in her quiet little neighborhood. A neighborhood she and he had chosen because of how safe it was. How sound.

"Donnie, do you hear that?" she asked as she rolled

over and stretched her arm across the bed, her ringed left hand searching for her husband's sleeping form. That was when the first real pang of fear gripped her heart, when she realized her husband wasn't there to wake and keep her safe.

It was his job to see what noises were in the middle of the night, his job to protect his sleeping family from all the scary things that went bump when the darkness was at its deepest shade of black. The noises had always ended up being feral pussycats or wayward raccoons. Until this night, that was. This dreadful, hateful night.

"Donnie?" she called out, the sleep instantly gone from her mind as adrenaline filled her veins. The screaming was clearer now, and she realized it wasn't just one house or two which the noises were coming from, but many, and all around.

"Mama?" Little Timmy called as he came running into her room. She could see the tears of terror threatening to fall because the moon was full that night, and the light from it shined in her bedroom window and danced in her oldest child's bugging, wild eyes. "Why are all the dogs barking, mama? And who's making all those yells?"

That was when Betty realized she heard dogs barking too. But there were other noises then, and some of the barking sounds would stop. And she knew what those other noises were, but they couldn't be. Not that many, and not from so many different places all around. There would be a loud bang, then a bark would cut off as if the dog was in mid-sentence. One after another after another. It was like there were people out there in her neighborhood silencing each person's pet as they came across it. It seemed like they were taking out these well-loved threats, ending them before they could attack or bite.

Betty jumped up from the bed, her legs entangling in the quilt, and she fell at Timmy's feet. He was full-on crying now, and her heart was beating in her ears. The noise of both those things was almost too much for her to bear when mixed with the cacophony of guns and screams of pain and fear and the dogs barking and being silenced from outside. It was too much for her to take in all at once, and so she made herself sit there for a second she didn't know if she could spare. Just long enough to center herself in that moment. Long enough to think about what she needed to do to make it through.

"Grab the baby, take Timmy and Nessa, and hide," she whispered as she pulled the quilt free. And then she whispered it again. "Grab the baby, take Timmy and Nessa, and hide." Just three things. Not so hard. So she pushed the rest of everything from her mind. She didn't want to think of what it was they would be hiding from. She didn't want to think about what was outside her house or why her husband wasn't here.

Down the hall, Nessa started screaming and the baby began to cry. Fear was replaced in her by something worse, something that turned her spine to jelly at the same time it turned her legs to steel. She knew she need-ed to get to them and quiet them before whoever was out there came into her home. She needed to keep them safe by making them invisible, so she grabbed Timmy up in her arms and ran.

"Nessa, come here, it's okay. Come to Mama," she called as her feet thudded into the hall, and blessedly her daughter's cries stopped at the sound of her voice. One less noise to mix into the symphony of the world around. One less sound to distract her from what she knew needed to be done.

In the baby's room, she sat Timmy on his feet and grabbed up her youngest child from his crib. The tiny baby's face was scrunched up as tears fell from his squeezed-shut eyes and ran underneath his chin. "Shush, baby, shush," Betty soothed and cradled him onto her chest, holding him there tightly as she grabbed up his yellow hippo blanket and turned back toward the hall.

"Mama," Timmy said, "what now?"

She heard the fear in her young son's voice, a fear she felt inside her own thumping heart, and as Nessa joined them in the small babe's room, Betty realized she had no idea. She had no idea, so she just stood there, rocking the baby. Hoping that the answer would come to her and praying the baby would stop its cries. Hoping her husband would suddenly appear and wishing with all her heart this was just some dream she could awake from.

As she stood in the middle of the baby's room, Timmy and Nessa standing there before her, their tiny hands clasped tightly in each other's, their eyes pleading up at her to keep them safe, a loud crash from downstairs made them all jump, and the baby's cries grew even louder in her arms. She knew then she was almost out of time and she needed to do something quickly to save her babies. Something smart and wise and brave.

But Betty had never felt like she was smart or wise or brave. She had never studied hard in school because she had never really cared about where she would go to college or about building a career. She had only ever wanted to do one thing for as long as she could remember, and that was to be a mother. She had only ever dreamed of holding babies in her arms and raising them into good humans who would make the world better because they were in it. To her, that was all that mattered.

Her older sister had been the one who lost herself in studies. Who had gone to college and became a surgeon and moved to New York City to specialize in some specific area Betty couldn't even pronounce. Some high-paying, high-stress career that made their parents proud. And so Betty had been lost in her shadow. She had been okay with that. Because by then she had met Donnie, and she knew her own life was ahead of her, her own dreams about to come true. And they had. They had. Until this night. This night that turned those dreams into a nightmare.

"Betty, run!" Donnie's voice came from somewhere down below, and then the sound of other men shouting at him, and she couldn't tell what they were saying because there were so many, all on top of the others. All mixed together. Her mind couldn't untangle the strings of their words. Then the sound of glass breaking and Donnie's screams of pain and all three children were crying now, and her mind went blank as her heart was filled with ice so cold she was afraid the baby would be able to feel it through her chest.

"Come on," she said to the two little ones as she turned toward the stairs leading up at the end of the hall. Timmy followed right after, dragging Nessa along by the hand, and the three of them, four if you counted the baby in Betty's too-tight grasp, ran toward the closed door at the end.

The noises from downstairs were getting louder, and

she knew soon she would hear footsteps on the stairs, but the thought of it was far away, as if her mind was numb. She wasn't even sure she was aware of where she was taking them. She felt more like she was on autopilot, as if she was watching this unfold from somewhere outside herself. Sitting in a theater built for one, the movie screen filled with horror.

She twisted the knob and opened the door, but as Timmy started to run up the stairs into the attic, she pulled him away and ran back toward her bedroom. Once there, she slid open her closet door, rushed her kids inside, and slid it shut again. The baby was still crying in her arms, and a shushing sound was coming from her lips, though it was just a reaction to the noise the small babe made and not some motherly choice she was making.

"I can't see," Nessa cried in her tiny voice, and Timmy pulled her closer to him to soothe her fears a bit while he waited to see what his mama would do next.

Betty pressed their shoulders down with her one free hand as she bent onto her own knees and shuffled underneath the hanging shirts and jackets above her head. All the way back and to the right. She fumbled over shoes and boots, and finally, she found what she was looking for.

There was a small, wooden square covered in the same painted white wood as the rest of the closet and hard to see if you didn't know it was there. If you moved it aside, it revealed a tiny room, a room built to hide a safe by the previous owner. It had once been a closet in the hall, her husband had told her, but the man had walled off the doorway and instead made it accessible from here, a fact she was very much grateful for as she crawled in clumsily with the baby in one firm arm and pulled in Nessa and Timmy right after.

It was hard to get the wood back over the hole just right in the darkness that filled this small cramped space, and she had to make Timmy hold the screaming infant as she tucked the piece back into its recessed place.

Finally, she felt they were as hidden as they could be, and she gently took the baby from Timmy's too-small arms and rocked him absentmindedly.

"He won't stop crying," Timmy said, and she sensed how terrified he was, and Nessa too. This room should make them feel safer, but with the baby wailing so, it felt more like a trap than a place to hide. More like a tomb.

"Sssshhhh, Blakey, shhhhh," Betty soothed and bounced the baby softly at her shoulder. "Ssssshhhhh."

"Hush, little Blakey," Nessa sang, though as quiet as a mouse, and Betty couldn't help but smile at her, even though she knew the child couldn't see. "Don't you cry. Mama's gonna buy you a punkin pie."

"Shush up, sister," Timmy scolded Nessa, though quietly and gently, and Betty felt him wrap his arms around her tightly as they pressed against their mother in the cramped little space.

"But they're gonna hear him," Nessa said, barely audible over the sound of the crying baby in Betty's arms. "They're gonna come." The fear was so thick in young Nessa's words that Betty's body flushed with panic.

Downstairs, Donnie started screaming, and the sound of laughter drifted up through the wood, even over the baby's too-loud cries. Betty bounced the baby harder in her arms, but just a little. She didn't want to hurt him, just make him stop, to make the sound that would lead those monsters to them end. But she didn't know what she could do to calm the tiny thing.

Suddenly, her mind filled with an idea, and she felt so stupid for not having thought of it before. So dumb. Betty lowered the baby into the crook of one arm, raised the ratty tee she wore to bed, and brought his tiny mouth to feed. The cries turned to whimpers and then silenced altogether as she felt the gentle tug and heard the softer sounds he made when he was eating, and both children sighed. Betty felt like laughing and crying all at once, but she knew she mustn't make a sound.

"We're all gonna be really, really quiet now, okay?" she said as low as she possibly could. She needed the children to hear, but she was afraid of her voice traveling into the hall. "No matter what we hear outside, we're not gonna cry or talk, not even a whisper. We can't let them know we didn't go into the attic. We can't let them know we're hiding. They have to think we ran upstairs."

She paused to listen, and once she felt confident none had come up to the second story, she continued on. "If we hear them running down the hall or in the closet tearing things apart, we can't make a single sound. Not one." Her words came quicker as she felt like she was running out of time, as if a giant hourglass was cracking and the sand was falling faster than it should. "We have to be braver than we've ever been. Nod your heads if you understand."

Both children's heads moved up and down against her arms as they were cradled in her lap, and the weight of them against her inner thighs caused her shaking legs to ache. She didn't know how long they would need to be here, how long they would have to hide. But she felt as if maybe they would be okay now. Now that the baby stopped his cries.

Downstairs, Donnie began to shriek and squeal again, sounds filled with such great pain Betty couldn't comprehend that it threatened to break her mind.

In her arms, the baby stirred, and Betty rocked her body the slightest bit, hoping to bring comfort to all three children and praying Blakey would stay quiet at her breast.

The screaming went on and on and on for what seemed like an eternity to them. The littles both had their hands above their ears, pressed tightly, trying to block it out. Betty put her free arm around them and hugged them as closely as she dared so as not to cause the baby to cry, and the three of them wept silent tears. Tiny whimpers escaped little Nessa, but they were almost too low to hear.

When the bang finally came that ended poor Donnie's life, all three jumped. But Betty was relieved. Relieved because whatever it was they were doing to him down there was finally over. He could be free from the agony of it. The torment. She didn't want to know what caused him to sound like some dying animal. She didn't want to know what they put him through to cause him to make those sounds, but she took solace in the fact it was finally over.

It was a relief that didn't last long, because when they jumped, it caused her nipple to fall from Blake's small mouth and the baby began to bawl. "No, sssshhhh, sssshhhh, sssshhhh," Betty whispered as loudly as she dared, desperately trying to get him to latch once more, wanting to soothe the babe before they came, for she felt like now that Donnie was surely dead, searching the rest of the house would be their next priority. Whoever *they* were.

"Mama," Timmy whimpered, and it was the only word he needed to say. It said everything there was to say.

Betty shut her eyes against the pitch-black space as she tried one last time to soothe her youngest child. But no matter how she positioned his tiny head or where she guided the nipple, he would not quiet. The baby would just move his head away and take in another breath to scream.

Her new dark world grew somehow even darker. Every sound came all at once but also in their own individual layers. She could hear all of it as if she was hearing everything on its own.

Nessa's tiny whimpers, so sad and low and lost. Timmy's worried breathing, hitching just a bit with each exhale, as if he was trying not to cry. To be the big boy. The little man his father always said he was with a wink and a rustle of his hair. The sound of unknown voices laughing in a room downstairs. Like best of friends just visiting and catching up.

And the worst of all of it. The worst sound of all. The sound like a hammer pounding nails into a coffin. The sound of helpless baby Blake screaming in his mother's arms.

Betty knew what she must do, and she hated herself for it. But what else was there? If she didn't stop the screams from filling this tiny space and spilling into the hall through the thin wall between, they would come. And what they would do to Timmy and Nessa, she didn't want to know. She couldn't bear it.

Betty did the only thing left to do. She made the choice to save the other two. She took her one free hand and placed it over little Blakey's mouth and nose, and she pressed. She pressed until the crying stopped, and then she pressed a little more.

She was filled with terror at the thought of taking her hand away now that silence filled the spaces in between their shallow, quiet breathing. She was consumed with fear at the thought that the poor baby's screams would resume. That the sound would make its way as if a beacon out and down and to the evil that lurked below.

Beneath her hand, the baby tried to jerk its tiny head, but she held it firmly still. A look of horror mixed with terrified desperation covered Betty's face as, inside her chest, her heart broke into a trillion tiny pieces. All her love for this child she held, begging her to stop. Her heart throwing itself down before her mind and pleading with everything it had to make her take her hand away. To stop this madness and let whatever comes be what it would be.

Little Blake waved his tiny fists and feet, and Betty held him even tighter. She didn't want her older children to know what she was doing, and the space was much too small to keep a thrashing baby from them for long.

"Sssssshhhhh, Blakey, shhhhhh," Betty soothed, and burning tears swelled and dropped from her sightless eyes. Sightless in this place devoid of light.

Her voice was as shattered as her heart, and she wished on every star she had ever seen or ever would see that he would calm now at her breast. That his little limbs would loosen and he would simply fall asleep and that she could take her hand away before it was too late. That his little chest would rise and fall in that steady way it had while she watched him gently slumber. That it wouldn't end this way for him. That his story would have another chapter.

She could feel Timmy pull Nessa into his arms and Nessa's arms wrap tightly around him in return. In her own, the baby's spit-wet lips rubbed against her palm, and his chest hitched as he tried to suck in air that wouldn't come. As he fought to simply be. As he fought to live and breathe.

Out in the hall, she heard them heading up from downstairs. Heavy boots on polished wooden steps. Her arms held the baby even tighter, but her shushing stopped. With each stair the bad folks took, the children jumped, and with each clump toward where they sat, the baby slipped a little closer to its end. To its forever sleep, and hopefully to dream.

Time for Betty seemed to slow as a frozen fist of anxiety slid down her throat, catching her breath inside her lungs and slipping its icy grasp around her heart. Chilly whisps ran up inside her mind and down her spine and to the tips of each and every finger and toe. She could feel the baby's heart beating rapidly against his frail little chest, then she could feel it start to slow. Bumbumbumbumbum bum-bum-bum bum bum... bum... bum...

Once more the baby jerked, and then he stilled, and one last bum fluttered against the inside of Betty's wrist. All was silent then inside their tiny hidey hole aside from shallow breaths coming from the two small children between her legs. Each was still holding the other as if they could fade away into the darkness at any moment if their grasps even loosened just a bit.

Outside, the heavy boots had made it to the top of the stairs, and they could feel the boards below them shake as the invaders ran down the hall.

Doors to all the rooms were slammed open and hit the walls, bangs that caused small whimpers from the kids that Betty didn't think could be heard from those making all that noise. Things were slammed and thrown and broken, ripped and torn. They could hear the noises of their home's destruction as if it was coming from all around them. As the door to her bedroom was kicked in and crashed into the wood on the other side of where they hid, she finally removed her hand from the dead baby's face and pulled those who were still living close into a hug. Their warm little bodies pressed against the baby's cooling one, and she held them all as close as she possibly could.

The sound of shouting drifted through to them, words they couldn't understand. Angry syllables barked out into the room at the same time as the sound of what she thought was her bed being flung into the wall. *Probably to see if anyone is hiding beneath*, she thought, and in her arms, her children shuddered.

"Sssssshhhhhh." She made the sound as silently as she could, just a whisper of a breath to give her children something calming to hold onto. Something soft. Something safe. She could feel their tears wetting warm into her shirt, and her own dripped down onto their wild-hair-covered heads.

As *they* rummaged through her room, her drawers, and the attached bathroom cabinets, she could sense them getting closer to where they hid. When finally the closet door was slid open so hard it rattled in its frame, Betty and her two remaining children held their breath. It was now that all would either end or keep on going. It was now they would either be found and dragged out with hate-filled hands or where their secret room would stay a secret.

Hangers filled with clothes were swept aside, and shoes were thrown about. Hat boxes filled with odds and ends were torn open and rummaged through, and the booted feet of men got closer. Still they held their breath, afraid now to let them out in case that tiny sound could somehow make it to the ears of their intruders.

Betty gave her kids a gentle squeeze, hoping to soothe them as much as she possibly could. She felt so helpless in that moment. So small. So vulnerable and cold.

Bam! They jumped as something large was thrown down onto the closet floor just outside the tiny hidden door. Inside her mind, she could see a hand reaching down to grab whatever it was that had been dropped, and in her mind's eye, she saw the hand pause as the owner looked up and happened to see the thin line in the wood that betrayed them. The crack that showed there was a door. A door to where they were. And in her imagination, she saw that hand move toward the crack and fiddle with it until it found a way to pry it open. And then she had to force her mind to stop, because where it would take her from that point was unthinkable, even more unthinkable than her dear husband lying dead upon the tiled floor downstairs. Or the lifeless little corpse she held, cooling at her chest.

After what felt like far longer than what it really was, the booted feet retreated, and the three of them resumed their shallow breaths. The people left the closet and then the room, and they could hear the sounds of them going down the hall, treating each door they passed the same as they had this one. And finally, Betty heard them take her bait and go up into the attic as she had hoped they would. Her plan had been to make them think that anyone who lived here had gone up there to hide and then gone out the window onto the little ledge.

She and Donnie often escaped up to that tippy top of their once-beloved home. They would wait until the children were all asleep, tucked away safely and soundly inside their little beds. Then they would grab the baby monitor and sneak up that same hall and those same shadowy stairs the bad men used. Up and up they would go, and they would sit upon the two old stuffy chairs they had pushed to face the window. They would talk about their days in hushed tones, even though there was no way the children could hear. Sometimes they would have a glass or two of wine or something harder, and sometimes they would bring a blanket out to that little spot upon the roof and smoke some weed Donnie would bring home from a guy at work. After, they would laugh and make the sweetest love up on that secret landing that nobody else could see underneath an entire sky of stars blazing just for them.

In the closet, Betty cried new tears, these ones just for Donnie and those times she knew they would never share again. In the closet, the children laid their heads against their mother's chest and fell asleep. The relief of them not being found was so great that it drained away whatever remaining energy they had. And in the closet, Betty held her three children as her ears continued to track the people in her house. She was praying to whatever god or gods there were that they would go onto that ledge and see the way she could have taken and think there was nobody left here for them to do whatever it had been that had made Donnie scream so much.

For there was a way on that landing upon their roof to sneak over to the neighbor's place. Their houses were built very closely together here, and the ledge where their window sat was close enough to the roof of the house next door to just hop on over. Though she had never been, and so had no way of knowing if there was a way down from there, she hoped they would assume there was. Whoever *they* were, she hoped it with all the strength she had left within.

The houses being so close was what had made that landing their secret little spot. It had provided that sense of privacy where the only things that could see them were the stars above. Those brilliant balls of gas that burned all those years away and sparkled just so they could see them do so.

Minutes seemed to pass as Betty listened. For her, it felt like eons came and went. She was relieved the children had fallen asleep in her one arm that was pulled around them tightly, and even though her feet and legs had fallen asleep beneath their weight, she held them as if to let them go would have them float away. She could hear *them* rummaging through some of the boxes upstairs, and she could hear their shouts as they looked, and every single part of her sat on this weird edge inside her soul. One side beckoned her to sleep, and the other side warned her to run. If she fell asleep, she knew she would fall and keep falling. The world would be a silent place and she would have no idea of knowing where the bad folks were who had forced their way inside her home. She would have no way of keeping her young ones safe if they came back around.

If she ran, she could maybe make it down and out. If they had left no one there to guard the stairs, that was. She would have to leave the baby lying here, left behind because she couldn't carry them all and flee. Not the way she knew she would need to. Her legs were numb, and moving them even slightly brought trembles of itchy pain that ran up from her toes into her thighs, and she knew they were useless, anyway. So Betty sat, fighting the urge to fall to either side, and Betty waited.

Finally, the boots came back down the stairs and down the hall. Her breathing caught again inside her lungs as she heard them move past their spot, just a couple pieces of drywall between their certain death and the worse that would happen before and their safety. Once she heard their feet stomping back down the stairs, their voices talking casually among themselves now that they perceived all threats to be gone from here, she forced herself to take another gulp of air, and another. Still, she waited. Fighting the urges to fall into the sweet escape of slumber or to go. And even after all sounds of them were gone and it would seem they had moved on to the houses down the street, she sat and listened, just in case.

She didn't know how long it was before she finally allowed herself to fall off the edge on which her mind was finely balanced. But when she did, she was grateful for sleep's comforting embrace. It held her as she held her children. And together, they let the world drift on as their minds tried to keep them safe in the only way they could—by blocking it all out and giving them dreams of brighter days gone by. Days they would never share again because parts of their family were gone forever. Suddenly and cruelly erased endlessly from their lives.

When Betty awoke with a snap sometime later, her head jerked back and hit the wall with a thud. Timmy and Nessa both jumped, and the baby almost slipped from Betty's sleep-slackened arm. She caught him just in time and frowned at how stiff the poor thing was, no longer yielding to the world around him. There was a little give in the baby's back, but his arms and legs were frozen and his little fists were forever clenched. She could feel them through the blanket she had wrapped him in.

She mourned that child, even then, in the beginning of the end of it. She wanted to scream and cry and let loose all the pain pent up inside her. Pain as frozen as his tiny little fingers were. And with the realization that what she had done could never be undone, a part of her soul died, too, the part that made it easy for her to laugh and love and trust.

"Mama, are they gone?" Timmy whispered, his voice so low she could barely hear it even though there were no other sounds. No barking dogs out there and no gunshots to silence them. No laughing men or screaming neighbors.

"I don't know," she whispered back, trying to keep her voice as quiet as she could, just in case. Because part of her wasn't sure they hadn't left someone behind. Someone to watch and see if there were people still alive. Overlooked and forgotten.

"Mama, I have to go," Nessa whispered then, just the tiniest bit louder, and fear suddenly rushed through Betty, a feeling of fire and ice all wrapped up together.

She couldn't let them out, not yet. She couldn't risk their lives. It wouldn't be worth the price she had paid to keep them safe if she let them out just to be caught. Just to be tortured and killed. It would have made the baby growing stiff against her own still-warm body a meaningless sacrifice.

"It's okay, baby, just go here," Betty said, so low.

There was a silence then as both her children thought about what that meant, their training not so old inside their minds that they couldn't remember the shame of going when and where they shouldn't. A shame their mother hadn't instilled inside them but was there, just the same.

"I can't, Mama," Nessa said too loudly, and they all breathed a sharp breath of fear in case there was someone out there who could hear. After a while, and after nobody came running up those stairs at the tiny sound of Nessa's words, she tried again, much softer. "I can't."

"You can, it's okay, I promise," Betty said, and as those words came from her drying lips, she realized that she, too, had to go. The pressure of it pushed down hard against her belly, and she sighed. They would all have to do that thing they knew they didn't want to do in here, just in case. And so, they did. Eventually, they did.

Betty didn't know how long they sat inside that room. The children grew thirsty and hungry, and the baby she held grew more rigid. They slept for times, and sat awake, each being as quiet as they were able. They cried and talked in hushed voices and consoled each other as best they could. She didn't know how long they sat, standing up every now and again as carefully as their cramping bodies would allow just to get the blood flow back into their legs and toes before carefully folding themselves back into their original positions.

Time was weird inside that pitch-black little room. Time felt like it was speeding by but going slower than it had ever gone. Betty felt like the world outside must be crumbling to dust as sunrises came and went and came again a million times over.

She also felt as if time must have stopped completely, because why hadn't anyone come? Why were there no sounds of police or soldiers rushing to their rescue? Why were there no sounds of other humans doing what they do when horror passes through? The sounds of people searching for survivors? When would that come? And why was it taking them so long?

"Mama, what's wrong with Blakey? He's been so quiet, and he feels a little cold," Timmy asked at some point in the middle of it all. She could feel his searching hands gently pressing upon his baby brother's cheeks and head.

"He's just sleeping, baby, everything's okay," Betty said, hating the lie but unable to admit to him the truth. Not wanting him to know what she had done, what she had had to do. Not wanting him to ever feel the weight of guilt that already threatened to consume her, even now in the early part of after. Not wanting him to ever have to hold it on his own two little shoulders. The weight of that single choice she had to make to ensure he and his little sister were safe. And his mom.

He didn't make a sound to let her know whether he

believed her lie or not. He didn't say a single word. But she could feel his hands still pressed against one cheek and rubbing slightly on one frozen little arm. As if he was trying to warm that tiny body she still held against her chest.

She didn't know if she would ever be able to let her baby go, even after. She felt as if she would carry him with her always. This tiny child who never had a chance. All the hopes she had for him, all the dreams, dead with him. Her little baby Blake. She remembered the night he had been born and placed into the same spot he was now. She remembered all the thoughts that ran inside her mind. All the what-ifs for his life yet to be lived.

Would he grow up to be a handsome man, just like his father? Would he have ambitions like her sister had? To be a doctor? Or would he work a simple job somewhere, building houses with his hands or teaching kids how to read and write? Would he marry well and have children of his own someday? A day that she had no idea back then would never come. And how it all would end by his own mother's hand. She would have been horrified and in full-on disbelief, the mother of that brand new baby sitting in that hospital bed not long ago. She would have said there was no way ever she could take his life, not even to save the other two.

But it had been a choice she made so easily when the time had come. A choice she now knew she would have made again a million times over if she had to relive that single moment. Because it had been him or all of them, and there was no choice in that, not really. Bu, still... Even though... That single memory would haunt her.

Finally, the sounds they waited for came drifting

through the walls. The sounds of helicopters and heavy trucks and people shouting words they could all under-stand. Even though, fear held them there in that tiny space that had been built to keep a safe tucked out of sight from would-be robbers. That tiny space that had begun to smell from the things they had to do while stuck inside. Not until a woman's voice came calling up the stairs was Betty able to move.

"Hello? Is anyone here? We're here to help." She knew the voice she heard was from a friend and not a foe, and tears of almost-happiness streamed down Betty's cheeks.

"Here! We're here!" Betty tried to yell, but her voice was hoarse and cracked, not from being overused but from the lack of anything to drink. Instead, she took her arm from around the older kids and started banging on the wall, and then Timmy and Nessa were as well, and all of them were screaming as best they could.

Rescue had come, and they were saved, even though the hardest times of all were yet to come. The living was the most difficult. The letting go.

The family that had gone to bed that night whole and happy would never be again. The baby that was now just a memory, and the husband and father that was now just a part of the times they used to know. And hardest of all, the mother's choice that had saved them each from an evil that the stories of what happened that dark black night told them would have been worse than anything they could ever have imagined.

But she would feel his weight forever after, against her chest. She would always feel his face against her palm. That choice she made seeped inside her heart and feasted on her soul.

Often, as she lay awake at night, cold and alone inside her too-big bed, she would hear him crying, and she knew. She knew he wanted her to join him. And she knew one day, she would.

# Borrowed Time: Damned to Hell 2

## Mike Salt

*Today*

Carol spent her entire life living for a single moment. Every choice she made along the way, whether planned or in reaction to events outside of her control, led up to this final act of violence.

The summer sky had disappeared behind the mountains surrounding Linkville and was replaced with a blanket of stars. These were the nights Carol tried to avoid. There were too many painful memories she would rather avoid, and often did.

The cool breeze off the lake brushed against her aging skin and lifted her grayed hair off the sweat on her face. She closed her eyes and listened to the sounds around her. The bullfrogs, the crickets, the birds. The sound of the lake moving and subtly crashing against her bare toes.

She was old.

Old enough to know the time was right.

Carol had wondered when that time would be or if she would even recognize it. If she would wait too long or miss the mark and never accomplish what she set out to do all those decades ago. What if she waited too long and this was all for nothing? That question was heavy on her mind throughout the years, the single question that made her drink to forget it all. Whiskey after whiskey, just so she could go to sleep.

Carol sat down on a log, reached her hand to the side, and retrieved a revolver she had sat there earlier. The metal was cold against her fingers. The price tag was still attached by a string around the trigger.

Carol removed the tag and loaded a bullet into the chamber.

"You don't have to do this," Babs said in her ear.

Carol didn't see him but knew he was there. He was the one that showed up the most, and honestly, she didn't mind the company most nights. Nights spent working the bar and dealing with drunk assholes. Scrubbing spilled beer and vomit from the countertops of Trappers Tavern. It was nice when he showed up. He was always around to lift her up and bring her back to the moment, even if he had a golfball sized hole through his temple, blood perpetually spilling out of it. His short, buzzed head matted with the dark red stain of the moment that brought them together. However, tonight she didn't want him around. She didn't want any of them around. She needed to have a clear mind, and she couldn't think straight with any of them around.

"You don't have to be that person anymore," Babs said

as his shadow appeared behind her.

She carefully snapped the revolver shut with a flip of the wrist and wiped a tear that was steaming down her face.

It was time.

*October 13, 1987*

Carol woke up to the sound of beeping.

With the sound came a rush of pain. Pain in her arm, which was in a cast and hanging to her side. Pain on the front of her forehead, which was wrapped with a bandage around her entire head. Pain in her chest, which with each breath made it harder to breath as panic set in. Her eyes were open, but her vision was blurred. As she tried to understand the situation, someone walked into the room and approached her bed.

Carol looked around the room. She didn't recognize it, but the pieces were starting to form. The bed was small and uncomfortable, metal rails on the side. The blanket was white and thick but felt stiff and scratchy. Tubes ran from her arm and into bags beside her bed.

She was in a hospital.

"Wh-wh-" Carol tried to talk.

"Don't," the female nurse said as she approached the monitors and jotted down some notes on a clipboard. "You've been out for a while. Let's get some liquids in you and get your vocal cords lubed up before we try and talk."

"What hap-happened?" Carol forced out.

The nurse didn't answer. She turned from the monitor and adjusted something on the bags. "I'll let the doctors know you're awake."

Carol tried to reach her hand out to stop the nurse from walking out, but her arm felt like it weighed a million pounds. It didn't move. Instead, she felt tears streaming down her face. Tears she couldn't wipe off as they ran down her face and chin and landed on her hospital gown. October 13th, 1987 was a day she would never forget. She opened her eyes and was in a new life she didn't ask for. A life she wasn't ready for. A life she would spend the rest of her life correcting. She just didn't know it yet.

The tears didn't stop as she lay on the hospital bed, recovering day by day. She didn't know the extent of her injuries until the doctor showed her. Two breaks in her right arm. Four cracked ribs. A fracture in her left eye socket and a rip down the forehead to the bridge of her nose. She suffered a traumatic concussion. Her face was swollen and bruised, her left eye so swollen it wouldn't open.

The doctors were certain she would be ready to leave the hospital in a couple of days, that she would be ready to go home with family and recover there.

The problem was Carol had no family left.

No one waiting for her. No one that knew she was even missing. Not any more. No, Carol would wait in the hospital bed until she could take herself home.

She didn't sleep much. She spent the majority of her days looking out the small window of her room from her bed. Not saying a single word, but inside her head was nothing but despair and horror. Flashes of memories that made her cry and want to die. Flashes of memories that filled her heart with regret and sadness. Flashes of memories that weren't fully processed yet and were just a piece of the puzzle as to why she ended up in the hospital in the first place. The scattering of glass. The screams. The crunching of metal. The sou—

"You look troubled," a man's voice said from the doorway.

Carol didn't move. The darkness of night had already arrived, and the window she was gazing off into was nothing but a black void.

The man moved from the doorway and into the room. He grabbed a small waste bin and dumped it into a larger bin on a cart. He placed a plastic liner around the empty bin and put it back where he found it.

"I know pain. Trust me, this will get easier," the man said as he closed the door behind him and continued on his way.

That was the first time she met Ben.

Over the next few nights, he would pop in and say a few sentences and continue on his route. "Pain is harder when you're alone," "Grief is a friend to depression," "You aren't alone." Whatever he said, something in his voice soothed Carol. She could tell he wasn't just saying things—he was broken too. Broken and reaching out a hand.

It wasn't until her final night that Carol finally rolled over as he entered the room. "What's your name?" she asked.

The middle-aged gentleman looked over at her and smiled as he went on with his routine. "Ben. Ben Frymore."

Carol adjusted her body in the bed. "What hurt do you know?"

Ben looked back at her, and his smile dipped for a moment before climbing back onto his face. "I know misery like no one in this hospital, ma'am."

"Please, call me Carol," she responded. "When does the pain stop?"

"For people like us? It doesn't," Ben answered. "However, it does get easier. It hurts less and less over time, and some day, years down the road, you will wake up and the first thought isn't about the pain. It won't be about it for a moment, and that's when it will finally get easier. Waking up and having a full shower without thinking about it. Another day you make it to breakfast or to your car on the drive to work. Or to lunch. Eventually the hurt isn't all there is. It's there, but it's no longer the only thing you have."

A tear streamed down her cheek. She brushed it away with her bruised arm. "What if I deserve the pain?"

Ben approached her bed. "Ma'am, no one deserves this type of pain."

"I do. I know I do," Carol said as the tears flowed at full force. "They died. I didn't. I'm here and they're gone. I need to feel this pain so that they never are forgotten."

Ben sat on the bed beside her and brushed a hand through her hair. His hands smelled like cigarettes and beer. "I understand. I do." Ben continued to brush his fingertips through her hair as she cried. He didn't stop until Carol broke down completely, and he leaned in and wrapped his arms around her.

Carol had been alone for all these days, no one to hold her and tell her it would be alright. No one to let her vent and scream at the world for being so unfair. Carol cried for countless minutes as Ben held her to his chest.

Finally, as the sobbing slowed down and the crying wasn't as loud, he spoke. "I lost my Bunny once."

Carol wasn't sure she heard him correctly, pulling herself from his chest and listening.

"I met my wife when we were sixteen, at the state fair. She was the cutest damn thing I had ever seen. Standing in line to get some tickets for rides with her friends. I was immediately in love. Not love like Hollywood wants you to believe, but real, actual love. I walked up to her and talked to her. Bought her tickets and asked if she wanted to go on the ferris wheel with me. I'll never forget the way her eyes looked as we rounded the top. She–"

Ben pulled away from Carol and gained his composure.

"We played some games with the extra money I had on me, which wasn't much at the time. I won her a stuffed bunny rabbit... And for the rest of our time together, she was *my* bunny." Ben smiled as the words left his mouth.

A stern voice broke into the room, a man with his own custodial supplies. "Benny, come on, man."

Ben nodded at the man and stood from the bed. "Well,

hopefully I'll talk to you again." As he walked out, Carol felt her heart racing. "What happened to your Bunny?" Ben didn't turn around; he paused for a moment before answering. "Nothing good."

*This is the opening chapter to the sequel for Damned to Hell. If you've read that book, you know that Rob spends a good amount of time with a bartender. A woman that he knew had a story to tell. This is that story.*

# The Calling: Mitch's Story

Jay Bower

*Fucking Gaige,* Mitch thought. Gaige was Gaige Penrod, Mitch's good friend who had convinced him to start up a band they were calling Cadaverous. Mitch hoped his parents didn't give him too much hell for the name. It could have been worse—Gaige really wanted to call the band Filthy Sticks.

As high school seniors, the band was made up of Mitch on bass, Gaige on lead vocals and guitar, Landon on lead guitar, and Nick on drums. Mitch was leery of them getting together, but he had been friends with all of them for so long that he looked at this as a last attempt to fulfill their dreams of being rockstars.

Cadaverous was slated to play the talent show at Brownsville's Pumpkin Festival in a few weeks. With the band finally choosing a name, Mitch decided to do something special. He only hoped there was enough time.

*Fucking Gaige*, he thought again, then climbed out of his car. *If the delay in coming up with a name means we can't have shirts, I'm gonna be pissed.*

He went to Star Threads, the local screen printer in Brownsville, with the intent to buy shirts for the band. He didn't really have an idea of what to put on them but guessed maybe just the name and, if possible, some cool graphic.

Mitch stepped inside the building and a friendly receptionist greeted him. "Hi! How can I help you?" she asked. Older, maybe in her mid-sixties, with short, curly gray hair and lines under her eyes, she seemed sweet and motherly.

"I'm hoping to buy some t-shirts for my band."

"Your band?" she asked. "That sounds exciting. Let me see if I can get a sales rep."

The woman picked up her phone and dialed several extensions, the look on her face growing from kind to worried.

She held the phone close to her body. "I'm gonna have to call Cheyenne. I...one minute." She offered a consoling glance, and Mitch wondered if maybe he was in trouble for something. Did he ask for the wrong thing? Did he break some kind of t-shirt buying etiquette? He had never done this before but didn't think it was going to be too difficult.

He heard the receptionist speaking in a low tone. Someone was yelling on the other side of the call. She winced, then hung up. She took a moment to collect herself. "Cheyenne will be out in a minute."

The hairs on Mitch's neck stood on end. Was it worth

dealing with a lunatic just for t-shirts? He had no idea who Cheyenne was, but if the receptionist's demeanor indicated anything, he was sure he was in for it.

A moment later, a woman stalked around the corner of the lobby, trudging toward him. She was shaped like a potato with twigs for legs. Bleached hair styled like she was in her twenties draped to her shoulders, though she was clearly as old as the receptionist if the creases in her forehead were any indication. The fake smile on her face made his skin crawl.

"Hi there," she said in a forced tone. "Let's see what I can do to help. Come on back." She turned and waved for him to follow. Mitch glanced at the receptionist, who seemed to say she was sorry with her eyes, then followed the woman back to her office.

Once inside, she closed the glass door and plopped down in her chair. Mitch sat across from her and fidgeted with his hands, wishing he had never have come there.

"What do you want?" she blurted out. No foreplay, no warming up. Just straight to the facts. Mitch swallowed hard before answering.

"I was hoping to get shirts for my band," he finally said.

She peered at him with steely blue eyes. "A band? You're just a kid. What the fuck do you know about music?"

Mitch sank lower in his chair. He had never encountered someone like this before. Who was this woman?

"Ok, then," she said. "How many shirts do you need?"

"Well, there's just four of us. So...four?" he said in a weak voice.

"Four! What the fuck kind of place do you think this

is? We need to do at least twelve to make it worth our while."

"But...ok then. Never mind." Mitch's heart sank. He didn't have a lot of money and didn't need a lot of shirts. For all he knew, Cadaverous might be a one and done band and after the Talent Show. They might never play again.

Cheyenne crossed her arms and leaned back, the poor chair squeaking as though crying for help. "I'll tell you what. I'll do the four shirts, but you need to do something for me. Deal?"

Mitch scrunched his eyebrows. "What?" He didn't like where this was going.

She leaned closer. The woman smelled of onions and Japanese Cherry Blossom, a scent his own mother often wore. As she peered at him, Mitch felt a heavy presence settle over him like a soggy blanket. It suffocated him. Alarms screamed in his head, but he lacked the ability to vocalize them. Cheyenne's eyes went from cold blue to the deepest shade of black he had ever seen in his life. A bolt of fear shot up his spine.

"You will serve him. Bring the boy to him, and you will fulfill your destiny," Cheyenne said. Her voice had dropped at least four octaves and was far more menacing than what it already was.

Mitch's eyes bulged from his skull. *What the fuck was this woman talking about?* he thought. If he wasn't held in place by an invisible force, he would have jumped from the chair and ran out of there. The band didn't need t-shirts that badly!

"Am I clear?" Cheyenne asked. "You can nod your head if you agree."

Mitch sat frozen in fear. *What the hell is all of this?* His heart raced wildly in his chest and his mouth went dry. It was like he had gone from zero to abject fear in .05 seconds.

"You will be the vessel. My feelers were out there seeking the chosen one, and they found him. You know the one I speak of. Make sure he finds the truth, and don't stray far from him."

Mitch opened his mouth to speak and was surprised his voice worked. "I...I was just wanting t-shirts. I don't understand what you mean."

Cheyenne laughed, and it was a deep, devilish sound as though her voice had sprung from the pits of Hell.

"You are getting so much more than shirts. You get the chance to serve. There aren't many called to do his bidding. Do not fail him and you might live."

The words from the creepy woman scared the hell out of Mitch. He hadn't come here for this kind of madness. All he wanted was to do something nice for the band. What did he stumble into?

"I don't know what you mean, but maybe I should just go. Forget I ever came in."

"Forget?" she replied. "Impossible. You have been marked. It is your destiny."

"You're crazy!"

Cheyenne grinned, then stood from her seat, walking slowly around her desk. Bending over so she was at eye level with him, she peered into his soul with her hollow, black eyes.

"Crazy doesn't begin to describe what you will experience." She placed her hand on his head. A sudden fiery pain wrapped itself around him, all of it extending from her touch.

He tried to scream but was forbidden by the invisible force that held him down. The scream echoed in his head, the only place it was allowed.

"That's it. Feel the fear. Does it taste wonderful?" Cheyenne asked. "You have no choice now. You've been branded with his presence. Bring the boy to him and your suffering won't be as bad."

*Suffering? What is this lunatic talking about?* Mitch fought the urge to piss his pants but didn't know how long he could hold out.

Cheyenne's touch continued to burn through his skull. He imagined it was only a matter of time until his hair caught on fire or his skin melted. When she placed both of her hands on his head, something happened.

The fire sensation immediately fled, and in its place was a frozen, lifeless feeling. It was like the light had been snuffed out and replaced with a terrifying emptiness. Something poured from her palms and snaked into his body. Coils wrapped around his brain, his heart, his lungs. He could do nothing to stop it; the sensation penetrated his entire being.

"That's it, feel him fill you up," Cheyenne said. The coils twisted and turned, pulling on his every muscle, attaching to his bones, fusing with his being. Mitch screamed in his head, but the voice was extinguished at last as whatever it was that infiltrated his body had finally taken root.

He was still there inside, but he also felt a barrier within. He beat against it with his thoughts until the realization that it was impossible to ignore finally settled in. Whatever she had done, it was now a permanent fixture. There was no doubt he could never get rid of it.

When Cheyenne removed her hands, it was like she had taken part of his soul with her. He longed for her touch again.

"There, that should do it," she said. "You are complete now."

Mitch didn't know what to say. Everything inside felt different. Rearranged. Scrambled. It was like the woman had taken his conscience and blended it until it changed consistency and reformed into what she wanted. He was still Mitch, but also something entirely different. The events faded in his memory until he felt like they weren't real.

He looked across at the woman. She was familiar, yet didn't know why. He came seeking her and needed something from her, that much he knew. What was it again? The struggle to think frustrated him.

Cheyenne took her seat and smiled at him. "So, t-shirts?" she asked.

Mitch nodded. He had come here for t-shirts for the band! That was why he was here, right? His mind was fuzzy, and he swore something felt different inside but he didn't know why.

"The guys are gonna love this," he said.

"Tell me more about this band. What's your name?"

"Cadaverous. We just came up with it."

"Interesting," she said. "I think I can do something to help. You only needed four, right? Let's figure this out."

Mitch was elated. The band would be so surprised by the gift; he couldn't wait to see the looks on their faces when they got the shirts. Things were looking up for him. Maybe Cadaverous might turn out to be something special after all.

# ACCURSED

## LEIGH KENNY

"Are you sure you don't wanna come stay with me for a while? I know you miss your sister. Heck, I miss her too. I can't lose you too, Kitty."

Cathy's rolled her eyes as she chewed on an already-ragged fingernail. With a huff of disgust, she picked a broken shard of purple fingernail polish from between her teeth. Of all the things in her life to die, she wished it had been that stupid nickname.

*Kitty.*

"No, Mom. Honestly, I'm fine," she said as she manoeuvred the phone to her other side, wedging it between her head and shoulder. Dropping heavily to the couch, she allowed her mind to wander as her mother continued to drone on. She knew her mom wanted her to come and stay, but not out of any kind of maternal instinct.

No.

Her friends had probably all grown weary of listening to the bereaved mother lament the daughter she had paid no heed to previously.

Neither of her daughters mattered all that much, but a dead daughter scored sympathy points that translated to free drinks with a few dinners thrown in.

If Cathy went to stay, her mother would just suck her dry and send her on her way. An energy vampire. That was her mom.

The thought sat heavily, and her skin prickled with unease as she scanned her surroundings slowly. Her mom wasn't the only energy vampire in her life.

As if on purpose, a heavy thump rattled the floorboards above her head.

A shiver darted along her spine as she raised wide eyes to the ceiling.

THUMP.

Against her better judgement, Cathy stood and moved toward the stairs, her fingers tightening around the phone. For once, she was thankful for her mother's self-centred monologue. It provided a comforting background hum without requiring any response. It made her feel a little less alone as she climbed, each step taking her closer to the box.

Closer to that god-awful thing that dwelled within its meagre depths.

Reaching the top, she stilled, straining her ears for the slightest of sounds. The house stood silent. Almost oppressively so.

"Are you even listening to me, Kitty?"

With a sigh, Cathy caught herself before her eyes could roll once more. She had work to do. She couldn't afford the eye strain.

"I'm listening, Mom. Actually, I'm kind of busy. Can I call you back later?"

Ignoring her daughter's request, the older woman picked up where she had left off as though the interruption never happened.

Cathy moved down the hallway, eyeing the box as she passed it.

It sat innocuously on the polished wood floor outside her bedroom door. No matter how often she moved it, that was the spot it always returned to, like a jailor guarding its prisoner.

Early morning sunlight spilled through the central window in her bedroom, and as she flopped onto her bed, Cathy watched with curious detachment as dust motes rose into the air and hung suspended in the golden glow.

Something moved in her peripheral.

Her eyes came to rest on the long cheval mirror that sat near the foot of the bed. Every hair she possessed stood to attention, and gooseflesh broke out across her skin. In the mirror's reflection, the thing from the box shuffled its way along the mattress, skittering toward Cathy like a giant, unwieldy spider, until she could no longer see her own reflection past the flowing mass of its dark hair.

She shuddered and slapped at her body, averting her eyes from the reflective surface.

There was nothing there.

Her gaze returned to the mirror, but the surface no longer reflected the room back at her. Instead, its surface was dark and shadow-filled, as though the glass had been removed from the frame entirely.

"Mom, I'm gonna have to call you back later," she murmured, hitting the *end call* button before her mother could respond. She tossed the phone gently onto one of the pillows, her eyes never leaving the black mirror.

Sliding from the bed, her bare feet hitting the floorboards with a muffled thud, Cathy crept toward the frame slowly. Something was wrong with the glass. As she reached out to touch the surface, her outstretched finger disappeared into the black void. She felt the oily texture and tried to withdraw her hand, but it clung to her skin in wisps. The frame wrinkled and swelled as she pulled, and a sob choked its way up her throat as she tried desperately to wrench herself free from the mass of black hair. A withered hand grasped at her wrist, its sharp nails embedding in the soft skin of her forearm as it pulled her closer to the mirror.

With a shriek, Cathy instinctively slammed her free hand against the rippling surface. There was no glass there, though. Just the cold, emaciated body of the woman from the box.

As she was dragged closer and closer, the darkness parted and the woman's alabaster face leered out at her from the curtain of wispy hair.

"Sisssterr. Mine."

That rasping voice felt like ice along her spine, and Cathy wept as she fought against the thing's inhuman strength.

Just as suddenly as it had grasped at her, the entity let her go.

Her head thumped heavily against the bedpost. As Cathy's vision faded, the rasping chuckle echoed in her ear.

The sun was high in the sky when she finally came around on the bedroom floor. She squinted at the glass as memories of that fiendish thing flooded her hazy senses, but to her relief, the mirror stood lifeless. Cathy pulled herself upright, frightened by her own gaunt appearance reflected back at her.

The past few weeks had hollowed her out. Grief had started the job, but fear was determined to end it. Knowing what the entity from the box had driven her beloved sister to was horrifying. She had hoped so badly to destroy the thing herself, but Cathy knew she couldn't carry on like this. It was using her sister's death as a means to break her, and she wasn't sure she was strong enough to continue. She needed rid of that accursed box once and for all.

Outside, the familiar rumble of the garbage truck grew as it turned onto her street.

She had an idea.

It was a terrible idea. A terrible, dreadful idea, but it was one that would finally absolve her of this curse.

She knew she couldn't take much more of this.

And still, she had to scrub the tears from her eyes. The gravity of what she was doing wasn't lost on her. Sometimes people had to do shitty things to protect themselves. Right?

Before she could talk herself out of it, Cathy slipped her feet into a pair of tennis shoes and grabbed the box from where it rested by her bedroom door. Her heart fluttered and her stomach churned as she jogged down the stairs and out through the front door. Her auburn curls streamed behind her as she marched across the lawn toward the garbageman.

"Here," she croaked, holding the box out. "Can you take this thing away?"

# Something's In the Water

## Debra Castaneda

There it was, right there in the picture. All the evidence Ken Bigg needed to confirm his theory: the scientists at Moss Landing were messing around with nature and creating hybrid sea creatures.

One of those damn things must have escaped and killed that sucker fishing near the pier.

Luckily, Marty over at the bait and tackle shop had taken a few photos before the paramedics rolled up.

The poor bastard had suffered a nasty wound—a puncture on the arm ringed in black, the skin around it a weird shade of purple. Made Ken queasy to see it, but he couldn't look away, either.

Later, he tried explaining his theory to the folks at Carla's restaurant, but they practically laughed him out of the place. He owned the bar next door, but everyone preferred to gather at Carla's thanks to the homestyle

Mexican food.

Peter, a retired state lifeguard and Carla's boyfriend, was first with a wiseass comment. "And here we go," he groaned.

Ken took another swig of beer and snapped, "Oh, come on. You don't think those scientists do stuff like that? Of course they do. Haven't you ever heard of a liger? A zorse? What about the grolar bear? Have you ever seen pictures of the geep?"

"What the heck is a geep?" Peter laughed.

Ken felt his face grow hot. "It's a sheep and a goat all mixed up. Now listen, I'm serious. Have you seen the size of those buildings they've got down there at Moss Landing? They're huge. What do they need all that space for? I tell you, they're doing some kind of secret experiments, and now one of 'em got out and did that." He pointed out at the San Refugio pier. "And I'm going to prove it!"

The smile vanished from Peter's face. "What do you mean prove it? How?"

Ken lowered his gaze and didn't answer. He hadn't meant to say that last part. How could he prove such a thing?

He glanced over at the windows. Dark clouds loomed over the churning ocean. Too rough to take his boat out, but if he hurried—

It was as if Peter could read his mind. The ex-lifeguard launched into a lecture, warning him to stay away from the water.

Ken folded his meaty arms across his chest.

"You'll see," he muttered.

With as much dignity as he could muster, he pushed

himself to his feet, regretting the three beers he had downed. He should board up his windows in case the meteorologists were right and a storm was headed for San Refugio Beach. The waves could break the windows and flood his bar and the village. It had happened before.

But first, he just wanted a little nap.

Laughter followed him out of the restaurant. Ken glanced over his shoulder and saw Carla watching him. She could be cranky and bossy, but she did look after him, badgering him to eat right and take his diabetes medication. Ken wondered if she needed someone to mother since she had lost her only son in a boating accident.

Instead of heading up to his second-floor apartment, he continued walking. Some fresh air would do him good. Wake up his brain.

In his weatherproof jacket, he fought against the wind as he walked toward the rock jetty, the salty sea air mingling with the musty seaweed strewn across the beach. When he reached the end of the path, he saw the receding tide had left a large pool of water in the sand several yards from the jetty.

Something was thrashing in the shallow water.

Ken stepped off the path, his orthopedic sneakers sinking into the wet sand. He stopped a yard short of the tidepool's edge.

The thing in the water surged toward him. Its head surfaced and Ken gasped. Round eyes regarded him with a human-like hostility that made him shudder.

Jesus, it was ugly. There was nothing normal about the reddish-black color of its skin. Something flashed in the air—a long tentacle. Between the bulbous shape of its head, that intelligent gaze, and the menacing appendage, Ken knew what he was looking at.

The hybrid. The creature that killed the man near the pier.

He had been right all along.

Behind him, a dog barked. He turned and saw an older man in rain gear, a large dog straining at its leash. Ken had to do something, quick, before the man let the dog loose.

"There's a dead pelican down here," he shouted.

The man grimaced, then waved. "Thanks for the warning. Cooper loves to play with dead animals."

Ken watched them leave, relief washing over him. It was a miracle no one else was around. The TV meteorologists had done him a favor scaring everyone away from the beach, and the locals were too busy preparing for the storm.

A white truck emblazoned with the city logo rumbled up, and a lanky figure in a yellow safety vest stepped out. Ken couldn't believe his luck. Benny worked for the city parks department and was in charge of maintaining the beach. His old buddy also shared Ken's distrust of the mainstream media and belief that shadowy groups were at work to undermine hard working people like them.

Ken's thoughts jumped to the steel vat at the back of his restaurant, the one he had picked up cheap to store the bar's paper goods, and he smiled.

He had his proof and a place to put it, and Benny was just the man to help.

Ken waved him over. Benny's long silver hair blew in the wind, his skin the texture of leather from years of working outdoors.

"Get ready to say goodbye to this tide pool," Benny said, walking up. "We're going to fill it in when we build the sand berm."

That was the city's go-to response to protect the businesses facing the beach. The sand berm helped shield the buildings from a high tide, but if things got really bad, it wouldn't stand a chance against a big storm surge.

Ken pointed at the tide pool. "Prepare yourself, Benny. There's something in the water that's going to blow your mind."

Benny frowned. "What the hell are you talking about?"

"I'm talking about those scientists at Moss Landing and their secret experiments. They created a freak hybrid, and it killed a man today."

Benny's eyes slid to the pool.

Ken watched in satisfaction as Benny's mouth fell open.

"Don't get too close. It's got a stinger or something."

Benny crouched down, one knee popping like a firecracker. "I gotta call my boss. They'll need to send people to come and pick this thing up."

"No!" Ken exploded. "You know what's going to happen? Your boss is going to call those crazies over at Moss Landing, the same ones who made that abomination. You think they're going to tell us the truth about it? Hell no. They're going to whisk it away and pretend it never happened. What we need is an independent expert."

"And how do you propose we find one of those?" Benny slowly stood, a hand pressed into his back.

Ken's heart gave a happy skip. "We gotta get it out of there and contain it until I can reach the right people.

This is big, Benny. Really big."

Benny glanced at the darkening skies looming over the ocean. "That thing's too big for your bathtub, Ken. And how the hell would we get it up to your place, anyway?"

"I got it all figured out. There's a steel vat behind the bar that can hold it. We back your truck across the sand, stick it in the back, and drive it over."

"Are you out of your gourd? You'll need sea water and—"

"There's plenty of water in the space below my place. All we have to do is run a hose down there and pump some up."

Ben's gaze was fixed on the tidepool. The water rippled and sloshed with each movement of the trapped creature. "You're forgetting something. That thing's deadly. How do you propose we move it without getting ourselves killed?"

Ken had been thinking about that. "We club it. Just like we do with tuna and swordfish, but not hard enough to kill it. We'll just stun it."

Benny rubbed the side of his face. "You make it sound so easy. I'm retiring in January, you know. We get caught and this could fuck the whole thing up."

Overhead, thunder cracked.

Ken gave his friend's arm a shake. "Nah. It'll be fine. Besides, we *have* to do this. Who knows what those scientists will get up to if we don't stop them." His voice trembled with indignation.

Finally, Benny met his gaze and gave a resolute nod. "All right. Let's do it and do it fast. I have a lot of shit to do before the storm blows in."

Benny trudged across the sand toward his truck. Ken watched as he closed off access to the beach, then set out orange cones to redirect traffic from Ocean Drive to a side street. Benny set out more cones on the stretch of sand leading to the tide pool.

When he was done, Benny drove the truck across the sand and parked near the tide pool, then rummaged in the bed and produced a large shovel.

"I'll do it," he said, tone bleak. "I'm in better shape."

Ken was in no condition to argue. He stepped back. "Don't let that tentacle get you."

Benny stopped abruptly, turned on his heel, and retraced his steps back to the truck. When he returned, he was wearing a heavy coat, a construction helmet, and work gloves.

He leaned over the tide pool, eyes narrowing at the creature gliding through the water, its smooth body sending ripples across the surface. As he steadied himself, gripping the shovel tightly, the creature's head came up.

Benny yelped, then lunged forward.

Ken's heart raced as he watched his friend teeter precariously close to the edge of the water, fearing he would fall in. But Benny brought the shovel down swiftly.

The creature went still.

"Please tell me you didn't kill it," Ken yelled.

Benny turned and glared. "I highly doubt it." He pointed to the truck. "Grab one of those tarps from the back."

Ken walked unsteadily to the truck, then returned with an armload of canvas. He tossed the tarp across the stretch of sand, keeping a safe distance from the creature.

Benny stepped into the water and wrapped the creature up.

For good measure, Benny wound duct tape around the lower section of the bundle. "Don't want it waking up and getting us with that tentacle. It does look like there's a stinger at the end of it."

When he finished, he signaled for Ken to join him. "Don't just stand there. Help me get this thing in the truck."

Together, grunting and cursing, they managed to haul their strange cargo into the truck bed. Ken guessed it weighed around 150 pounds, about the same as the college kid who worked at his bar.

The truck bumped over the sand. At the back of Bigg's Bar, Benny backed up until the cab reached the patio.

Ken hoped Carla wouldn't come out to investigate. But she was short-staffed and probably too busy to stick her nose where it wasn't wanted.

With unsteady fingers, Ken locked the patio gate behind them. No one could see a thing. Together, they cleared out the paper goods from the vat. Then they ran a hose from beneath the building and used a hand pump to fill the vat with the sea water that ran under the row of buildings.

As water sloshed over the sides of the container, they lowered the bundle inside. Kenny unclipped a utility knife from his belt and sliced through the tape, releasing the creature from its confines.

Both men instinctively moved away. It didn't move.

"Maybe I killed it after all," Benny said.

"Nah. Give it a few moments."

Sure enough, the water began to churn. Seconds later,

a bulbous head emerged and, just as quickly, disappeared back into the water. A tentacle eased up over the side, exploring its surroundings.

Ken jumped back, dragging Benny with him.

"You got a cover for that thing?" Benny asked.

Ken looked around, suddenly dizzy. Jesus. When was the last time he ate something? Had he forgotten his morning insulin?

Benny spotted the lid leaning against the patio wall.

Ken eased himself into a plastic chair. "I need to take a breather."

Benny frowned. "You really got to get a handle on that diabetes, Ken, or it's going to be the death of you."

"Take a few pictures for me, will you?" Ken asked, holding out his cell phone.

Easier said than done. After getting hit on the head, the creature was more interested in hiding than posing, but Benny managed a few shots before securing the lid and punching a few air holes in it with his knife.

"Not big enough for the tentacle to get through," he said when he was done.

The thing inside bashed against the side, but the lid held.

It wasn't going anywhere.

The radio in Benny's truck crackled to life. Ken was only half-aware of Benny slipping out of the gate, and then he was standing in front of him, a look of concern etched on his lined face.

"That weather forecast just got a whole lot worse. You got anyone you can call to help you board up? I'd do it, but I won't be getting a lunch break."

Ken gave a vague nod. "I'll figure it out." He paused.

"And thanks for your help." Like Benny had just helped him unload sandbags instead of a deadly hybrid sea creature that would do God-knew-what if it got loose.

Ken lay on his couch, staring up at the ceiling. The last day—or was it two?—had been a blur. He had contacted his favorite radio station. A reporter had arrived, gaped at the pictures on Ken's phone, then at the vat rocking back and forth on the deck, and hurried away promising to cover the story.

The meteorologists were right for once. The storm came and with it a surge of water that flooded his bar and the other businesses along Ocean Drive. Ken was trapped, probably along with everyone else who had ignored the evacuation warnings. He guessed maybe a dozen other people could be holed up in their second-floor apartments.

With all the creaking and groaning, Ken was afraid the wind and waves may have destabilized the entire structure.

And there he was, stuck, shaky all over, too weak to get to the bag of Skittles stashed in his desk drawer.

As consciousness began to fade, his thoughts drifted to the creature in the vat. The storm surge had probably knocked the lid loose and the creature was likely free. Ken wasn't a religious man, but he prayed it had gone out to sea. The last thing anyone needed was that monstrosity loose in the flood waters gushing through the village of San Refugio.

He really should have warned somebody.

# The Man in the Top Hat

## Devin Cabrera

The streets of Briarwood were quiet.

They always were, save the random sounds of a dog barking at a possum that happened to scurry across a yard at night.

Briarwood was a place where no one locked their doors at night. Crime was minimal to nonexistent, and any discipline that needed to be applied to the average schoolboy who decided to act up was taken care of inside the home, usually with a few swift smacks with a belt.

Drew had recently been on the receiving end of one of those beatings.

He had decided to blow a spitball into Macy Ray's hair earlier in the day, which had sent him to the principal's office. He was only trying to get the girl's attention because he found her attractive, but apparently, a giant wad of paper soaked with his saliva wasn't the best way to tell her.

His father had been called, and he had waited outside the principal's office while the balding man inside told his dad of his actions. He could hear his father promising to take care of it and that he would have a good talk with his son when he got home.

Drew knew what a talking to meant, and it usually had nothing to do with words and more to do with the sound of his father's belt scraping the loops of his pants as he slid it out in one swift movement.

He had been through this all before, and no matter how many times his father beat him, he would always find some way to get into trouble again.

His father had taken the cigarette out of his mouth with his free hand and stubbed it out with the heel of his shoe into the carpet, leaving a burn mark that only added to the black craters that pocked the fabric. With his other hand, he brought the end of the belt against Drew's bare ass until the boy promised he would never act up again.

They both knew it was a lie, and Drew was already thinking of new ideas to get Macy's attention, but he took his whooping and went to his bedroom.

He stayed there, skipping dinner as part of his punishment, laying on his bed and staring up at the ceiling long past the point at which the sun had gone down.

The town around him grew quiet at night, and nothing was going on to distract him from the thoughts that swirled around his head.

His parents had gone to bed long ago, and he could hear the sounds of his father's snores shaking the walls from a few rooms over. He turned over on his side and shut his eyes, covering his ears with his pillow.

Because of this, he was unable to hear the screams coming from next door.

After a few moments of trying to will himself to sleep, Drew saw red through his eyelids as a light shined on him.

His eyes shot open, and he realized the light was on in the room adjacent to his in the house next door.

That's odd, he thought to himself. His neighbors were usually pretty religious about keeping their lights off at night. The father of that household was cheap and demanded no electricity be wasted. He also wasn't against using his belt on any child who decided to turn the lights on at night, so the kids typically listened to him.

But something was different this time. Something felt off, but Drew couldn't put his finger on it.

He removed the pillow from his ears and listened, but he couldn't hear anything over his father's snoring.

Rolling his eyes at the man, Drew knew he wouldn't be able to sleep with all the new questions rolling around in his head. He removed his blankets and stepped onto the carpet, feeling the fibers make their way through his toes.

He walked over to the window and looked out.

The neighbors' window was covered with a curtain, so he couldn't see what was happening on the other side.

Using his father's snoring to cover up the noise, Drew slowly lifted the window, placed his arms on the sill, and rested his chin against them, listening for any sounds coming from inside the house next door.

At first, there was nothing.

Drew was about to close the window and go back to bed. But then he heard something.

Bang. Bang. Bang. Bang. Bang.

Drew's ears pricked up.

It was the sound of heavy footsteps as if somebody was running through the house.

And it was getting closer.

Drew kept staring at the window, comfortable it was dark enough in his room he didn't think he would get caught peeping if someone were to look out at him.

Suddenly a woman's shadow appeared on the curtains, which grew darker as she approached the window.

Drew instinctively stepped back until only one of his eyes peered around the window frame.

He wondered which of his neighbors was in the room across from him and why they were running around this late at night.

He was thinking about that when another shadow appeared behind the woman.

It was the shadow of a tall man who was definitely *not* his neighbor.

Drew knew this because of one distinct feature the shadow contained.

The man's shadow was wearing a top hat.

Just then, there was a scream as the man reached the woman. Their shadows fought each other on the curtain. The woman tried to break away from the man and dove for the window, grabbing the curtain as she did so.

The curtain ripped away from its rod, and Drew heard the woman scream just before the man swung a giant mallet down upon her body.

The scream cut off very quickly, and the shadows on the curtain were replaced by blood splatter on the window. Through the gaps in the blood, Drew could see the man swinging the mallet again and again until the window was entirely covered in the dark red liquid, pooling and dripping slowly down the glass.

Drew took another step back.

He didn't know what to do. Should he wake his parents? Should he call the police?

He was still thinking over his next move when he saw a shadow on the window grow very dark.

Then a long, skinny finger drew a circle in the blood.

Drew stood riveted to his spot on the floor, unable to breathe as he watched the events unfold before him.

The man moved his finger a few inches to the left, then drew another circle in the blood. He continued a few inches lower, then made an upward-facing arc, creating a smiley face in the remnants of what used to keep Drew's neighbor alive.

Drew watched in horror as the man pressed his face against the glass, lining his face up with the one crudely drawn on the window. His smile widened as he saw Drew watching.

The man was Jones Jepsen, a notorious mass murderer who had been terrorizing the streets of Briarwood for the last few days, and his eyes were trained on his next victim.

Jones raised a hand to the glass, and with one long fingernail, he tapped on it.

Tap. Tap. Tap.

Drew felt the blood in his veins turn to ice as his eyes met with Jones's.

He saw nothing in them that would represent a human soul. There was no regret for what he had just done, only hunger for his next kill.

Drew shifted his weight, preparing to make a run for it, and it was almost like Jones sensed the movement coming.

In an instant, Jones moved away from the window, his face covered in the blood of his last victim.

Drew knew Jones would be coming to his house next to kill the person who witnessed the murder next door.

Jones was fast, and Drew had two options at his disposal that he could think of. He could either run to his parents' room and wake them up, convincing them a mass murderer was next door and was coming to their house next, or he could run downstairs and lock the doors and windows before Jones got there, potentially saving all their lives and giving the police enough time to get there and handle it.

Drew paused outside his parents' room, the sound of snoring rumbling loudly on the other side of the door. He knew what he had to do.

Drew turned and bolted down the stairs, jumping over the last six steps and hitting the ground hard. He ran to the front door and turned the deadbolt in place, breathing deeply as the lock latched. He ran to all of the windows in the kitchen and living room, making sure they were locked. Then he boldly peered out from behind one of the curtains.

He stared out into the night, looking around desperately for the killer he knew was outside.

Jones wasn't on the street.

Drew ran to the other side of the house, facing the

neighbors' home. Once again, he peered through the curtains, trying to find the man responsible for his neighbor's murder. He couldn't see the man anywhere, but the front door of their house was wide open, swinging on its hinges as if somebody had just made a quick exit.

Drew heard a loud creaking sound coming from the back of his house, and the hairs on the back of his neck rose as he realized what he had missed.

He had forgotten to lock the back door.

Drew ambled toward the back of the house, holding his breath so as not to be heard. After what felt like ages, he got to the wall near the back door, pressing his back firmly against it.

The back door was in the mud room, on the other side of the wall, and Drew could feel the cold air coming in through the open door.

He reached down with his right hand, feeling for something he knew to be kept in that spot. His fingers tapped along the wall, and he cursed himself with every noise he made. Finally, he felt a long, smooth handle and wrapped his hand around the Louisville Slugger he kept there for whenever he wanted to hit the ball around the backyard.

Feeling a little safer now that he was armed, Drew took one final deep breath, working up the courage to move. Then he jumped out from behind the wall, brandishing the bat in front of him, toward the intruder.

Except there was nobody there.

The door creaked on its hinges as a soft breeze blew through it. It just hadn't been closed all the way from the person who had come through it last. Drew quickly shut the door and locked it, stepping back from the glass and looking around for the man he knew was out there somewhere.

Through the moonlight that filtered in through the trees bordering his backyard, he could make out a few things: the grill his father spent much of his time drinking in front of, the patio furniture his mother relaxed on when the sun finally made its way out from behind the clouds, and a few balls he had forgotten to bring inside. He made a mental note to pick them up before his father saw them and reprimanded him for leaving his stuff outside.

But Jones was nowhere to be seen.

Drew let out the breath he had been holding, and he remembered the scene that had unfolded in front of him at the neighbors' window. He had to wake up his parents and let them know a killer was on the loose nearby and they needed to call the cops.

Drew returned the bat to its place and ran up the stairs.

He paused outside his parents' doorway, raising his hand to knock.

Drew could hear his father snoring inside, and he knew the man would be pissed if he woke him up. His father worked early hours and didn't like his sleep interrupted before the alarm clock went off. Waking his father in the middle of the night would usually mean a whooping for him for sure, but as he thought of all the blood on the window across the street, he knew these were extenuating circumstances. He hoped his father would understand.

Instead of knocking, Drew turned the handle and

pushed the door open.

The snoring grew exponentially louder, and Drew could see the lumpy shapes of his parents under the blankets on their bed.

*I hope they're decent*, Drew thought as he walked to their bed.

The blankets were pulled over their faces, which he thought was odd. He continued anyway.

Drew shook where he thought his father's shoulder should be, but the snoring continued. There was no response from his father that hinted he knew his son was there.

Drew shook the man again, a little harder this time, but something strange happened when he pulled his hand away.

It came back wet and sticky. When he brought it to his face, he realized it was covered in blood.

Drew felt his own blood run cold, and he grabbed the edge of the blanket and yanked it back. What he saw made him fall to the ground, his hand covering his mouth in shock.

His parents were dead.

Both of their faces had been beaten to a pulp in their sleep, pieces of their skulls splattered on the pillows, soaking the sheets with a deep red stain that would likely never come out.

They never even knew what hit them.

A loud, wretched snore rang out from the corner of the room, and Drew's head spun around so quickly he thought he would have fallen to the ground had he not already been there.

Jones stepped down from where he was standing on

the dresser, his mouth contorting as he once again mimicked the snores of Drew's father.

The area was bathed in darkness, and Drew hadn't noticed when he came in.

Jones stepped forward into the moonlight pouring in from the window. He wore a dark trench coat and a top hat on his head. In his hands he swung a carnival mallet covered in the fresh blood of Drew's parents.

Drew's eyes traveled from the mallet to the man's face, which was the scariest thing of all.

It was pale and covered in specks of blood and brains. But the worst part was the smile that reached both ears, the smile that said he knew what he had done and was enjoying it.

It was a smile that said his fun wasn't over.

# THE NEED

## DE MCCLUSKEY

Vincent looked out his window as a shiver wracked his body. He could feel it start in his bones and work its way out towards his flesh, where he was instantly covered in a rash of goosebumps. He regarded his hand holding back the curtain and marvelled at just how much it shook and how much he must be used to it, as he couldn't even feel it.

He relieved himself of a long breath. He had vowed he wouldn't ever let it get this far again, yet here he was, in a dump of a room, in a dump of a house, in his dump of a life.

His mouth was dry, and there was an ugly, sour taste in the back of his throat.

He had been at this long enough to know exactly what that taste meant. In days gone by, he had enjoyed it, embraced it even. However, now that everything in his life had grown old, far too old, too soon, he hated the taste as he knew exactly what it meant.

He needed a fix.

Which in turn meant he would have to venture outside.

His stomach twisted and churned at the thought. He used to visualise this feeling as excited butterflies in his stomach, fluttering at the adventure they craved. Now he thought of them as black death beetles, crawling and stomping around his stomach, feeding on all the shit that was inside him, making him sick, ill, and worst of all, weak.

The thought of going out, heading off into that cold, unforgiving street was enough to make him succumb to the cramps, to the agonising knives that pierced his flesh, cutting him into a million ribbons, turning his insides out.

He closed his eyes and visualised a life without this *shit* in it.

It brought a thin smile to his damp, pale face.

It was just a moment's respite from the horrors of this life. *All of my own choosing,* he cursed. The curse was at himself. He had chosen this. It was his selfishness that made him what he was today, what he had been for too long. The promise of the highs, back in the day, beat the lows he knew he would feel every now and then. "When you hit a low," everyone told him, "you just need another hit. Then boom, you're back on the high again."

It was all so simple back then.

But then there had been more of them. His friends, he grinned. All of them as close as brothers and sisters, all sharing a seemingly unbreakable bond.

A bond that stayed unbreakable, until it broke.

He opened his eyes again. That vison had turned on him. *Why am I surprised? Everything turns on me.*

His friends, all of them were gone now. His life was pretty much an unbearable hell, his cravings, his addictions the only things that stuck around when everything else withered and died.

The twilight of the day was warm. He knew this because it was the middle of summer. A time he always thought of as *his.* It had been the time of revels, of all night parties and festivals. Everything had been theirs then; no one could have taken it from them. Only, it had been taken. The need had overtaken any enjoyment in his life. It had overwhelmed his friends, and one by one, they withered on the very same vine they tendered.

He had tendered to the same vine. He was *still* tendering to it. *Or is it tendering to me?*

This was a horrible thought.

Indeed, the night was warm, but he was cold.

Cold wasn't even the word for it. He was freezing. He felt like Death himself had come and touched him with one of his icy, skeletal fingers. Another small smile cracked his thin lips. He longed for death to embrace him. He welcomed it, but he was too scared to do anything about it.

His friends called to him in his dreams. They told him they were free, they were happy, bathing in the sunlight of an afterlife beyond his cowardly grasp.

He knew he would have to go out into that unwelcoming street, very soon. The twilight would protect him. That magical time, the one between day and night, had always been his favourite time, long before he yielded to the demands of his addiction. He treasured the magic of it, the swirling light cavorting playfully with the oppressions of the dark.

None of this was helping his situation. He needed to go out there, and he needed to do it now. If he waited any longer, it wouldn't be safe. The street held too many mysteries to him. He could feel the eyes of his neighbours every time he ventured out. He knew they knew what he was. He was something to be left alone, something not to be trusted.

He was a stinking junkie.

Only, he was more than that.

He chuffed at the thought of just being a junkie. *I wish it was just that. I wish it hadn't gotten this far.* He knew wishes were not going to get him what he needed, that they were like the stars in the Heavens, unreachable.

If he left now, he could make it to the docks at the end of the street. There he would be able to find exactly what he needed. He would be able to find *whom* he needed. They would be there. As long as there was a market, there would be pushers, sellers, dealers of slow death.

It was just the way things worked.

He grabbed his coat from the back of the door and slipped into it, grimacing as it pressed his damp clothes against his even damper flesh. He thought about not taking the coat, but he knew he would need it.

Even in the warmth.

A warmth he didn't think he would ever feel again.

As he grasped the handle of the door, the one he knew would expose him to the dangers of the street, the one that would expel him from the safety, the sanctuary of his dingy, little abode, his stomach twisted. Another cramp tore through him. This one began in the pit of his stomach, before it ripped its way through his entirety. He cried out. He didn't know if it was a scream or a yell, or even if he had stayed silent, and he didn't care. He looked at his hand; it was still grasping the handle as if his very life depended on it.

He felt like it did.

He had very little strength left. He never let it get this bad. *Stop lying, Vincent,* he chastised. *You tell yourself that same shit every time this happens. You've been here before, and you'll be here again, because you're pathetic. You're weak, you stink, and you're not even a shadow of the man you were before all of this.*

He took in a deep breath and pulled the handle.

*Fucking junkie!*

The door opened.

*Scum!*

The fresh air hit him.

He tasted it and stepped outside.

He checked his pocket. He had money. As long as he had that, he had everything he needed to get his fix, his drug, *his fucking hit.*

The taste on the back of his dry throat was screaming at him as he looked up and down the street. It nagged at him like an old wife, reminding him what a disappointment he was.

The street was empty, just as he knew it would be at this time. It was not a sociable time. The people in these mean streets were not gregarious at the best of times. He was glad of the seclusion; he needed it, revelled in it.

With a quick look to the sky, he noticed the deep purples were particularly deep, and the thin clouds were dark and brooding.

The sky reminded him of himself.

He pulled his collars closer around his neck, combating the wind pinching at his cold face. He took another breath and closed the door. He locked it. He knew what the people on this street were like. Even if he couldn't see them, he knew they were there. They would be ready to attack him, to beat him, to steal whatever was stealable from him. He had nothing to steal; all he had he was wearing, but they wouldn't care about that.

He took another look up and down the street before making his way down the gentle slope towards the docks, about a quarter of a mile away.

He walked slowly. He didn't want to attract any attention to himself. The velvety darkness suited his purpose. It hid his identity, hid his purpose, but mostly it hid his shame. He cursed his carefree youth. He wanted nothing more than to travel back in time, to warn his younger self of the dangers of what he was doing. He knew this would have been a fruitless mission as his younger self would have just told him to fuck off and mind his own business.

He saw himself as a kind of Ebeneezer Scrooge character, attempting to cajole his younger self not to make the same mistakes.

He might have laughed had it not been so sad.

The docks were just ahead; his short walk felt like a thousand miles. So far it was uneventful, and he thanked whatever god it was that looked down on wretches like him.

He watched as some obstacles appeared in the gloom before him.

It was an older couple. They braved the nasty street to

walk their, no doubt beloved, dog. He wanted to cross the road, to get onto the other side, before they could attempt to greet him or before their dog sniffed him. He longed for neither forms of scrutiny. The rejection from humans and animals alike would do nothing for his sensitive demeanour.

He hunched his shoulders and buried his face deeper into the shadows of his collars.

"Hey there," the elderly woman greeted him. "Don't mind old Scratch there. He's just a bit too friendly."

He looked at the couple, then down at the dog. He craved neither of them. He just wanted to get where he was going, get what he needed, and get back home to do what had to be done. He offered a non-committal, "Huh," before moving his leg into the direction of the dog, trying to ward it off him. He needn't have bothered as the dog had already sniffed him and decided this human wasn't worthy of his attention.

"How rude," the woman muttered as he continued shuffling along the street. "Come on, Scratch, lets get you home."

*Yeah, fuck off Scratch,* he thought with no humour in it.

His body felt as if it was falling apart. His legs felt like one tonne weights were attached to them, and his arms and shoulders shook, almost uncontrollably. He also would consider himself lucky if he didn't have to stop in a shadowy location and purge himself, possibly from multiple orifices.

This he knew he wouldn't do; there were limits, even for him.

The stink of the street drove him on, towards the

heavier industrial stink of the docks. There were always bangs and booms coming from this location, no matter what time of the day it was. Right now, there was no reason for it to be any different.

Each crash brought about more anxiety.

Each twist of anxiety brought about another cramp.

Each cramp he thought might have been his last, the very last of anything. He genuinely thought they might kill him.

He wished they would.

But they wouldn't.

He slowed his pace as a police car flashed along the deserted road. Its lights were flashing, but the siren was off, presumably in respect to any noise pollution it might cause the residential homes at this time. Understanding the police seldom came down this way alone, he ducked into a shadowy recess to wait out the inevitable second-car pass.

Less than a minute later, it flashed past.

He waited a few more moments before gritting his teeth and stepping out of the shadows.

"I've got what you need!"

He didn't know if he imagined the voice or if it had been real. In his current mixed up state, he couldn't even be sure if the police cars had been real.

"What?" he hissed, turning into the darkness.

"I said, I've got what you need."

A figure emerged from the darkness of the entryway behind him. He hadn't even realised there was an entrance there.

"How do you know what I need?" he asked the newcomer. He was looking into the darkness, attempting to see who it was he was talking to.

A silhouette emerged. It was lurking on the boundary between the dark and the light, a little like he had been doing. The shadow laughed. "Have you looked in a mirror lately?" he asked as he stepped out of the darkness, into the semi-darkness of the twilight.

The man was bald, and there was something about his features Vincent didn't like. He couldn't put his finger on what it was, he just didn't. "You're a hoot, but you didn't answer my question," he replied, trying to sound like he was desperate and terrified at the same time. "How do you know what I need?" His dry throat was raging now, and the nasty taste was back on his tongue. He dreaded to think what his breath smelt like, but that wasn't his problem.

"You think you're the only one around here with a need? You're my third so far."

*Three?* He hadn't thought about any others in need. A low-level panic bloomed in his stomach. *Would he have enough left for me? Enough to satiate my craving?* "Have... have you got any left?" Vincent stuttered, the vile taste in his mouth almost making him baulk.

The stranger laughed, leaving a smirk in its wake. "You got funds?"

He looked up at the sky and shivered.

"Oh, you've got it bad, haven't you?" the man asked, the smirk growing in stature.

"I've got funds," he replied, digging his hand into one of the deep pockets of his dirty mac. He pulled out a wad of notes and offered them with a shaking hand.

"I never told you how much I want for it."

"That'll be enough," he growled. The violence in his

voice took the man by surprise, knocking the smirk from his face, just for a moment, before it reappeared, stronger than ever. He took the money and stuffed it in his pocket without counting it. He put his hand inside his jacket and pulled out a small, rectangular package. It was wrapped in brown paper and looked purposefully anonymous. Just the way he needed it to be.

"You better run along now," the stranger grinned. "It's getting a little... late, isn't it?"

Vincent looked up at the sky. The clouds were thinning, and the sky could be seen between them. He swallowed again, issuing a dry click in his throat. The weight of the package gave him a confidence he hadn't had moments before. He scowled at the stranger, who stepped back into the darkness, nodding as he melted into the obsidian. All that remained was a dark chuckle.

Vincent looked at the sky again.

The man was right. The twilight was waning, and it would no longer be safe for him on the street. He still had to climb the uphill street before he was safe.

He looked back at the man. There was no longer any sign he had been there in the first place.

He fixed his collars and set off back the way he had come. His pace was quicker, in time with his racing heart. He needed to get home as soon as he could. The package was calling to him, whispering him promises that everything would be alright, all he needed to do was get home and it would make everything good again.

He knew they were empty promises, but they were all he had. The thought of making his way up the street terrified him.

In the grey light, he could make out his door. It was

the only red one on the street.

He sped up again, his whole being focused on that door.

That was when he saw them.

The old couple with their dog. They were walking back towards him, looking at him, leering at him. They were grinning. There was real malice behind their strange, glowing eyes. Even the fucking *dog* was grinning at him. He crossed the road, hoping to avoid them. Something about this side of the street didn't feel as safe as the other did, but it was something he would have to deal with, at least until the freakish couple passed.

"Filthy cunt," the old woman hissed.

Vincent looked at her, his jaw falling open.

"Die, you vile scum," the man spat.

Their mouths were too wide to be natural, too many teeth inside.

"I'll bite the *fuck* out of you," the dog hissed at him. He had to double take at this insult.

He shook his head and blinked, hoping to clear his head of this horrible vision. As he opened them again, the couple and the dog were still there, still leering at him. A long snakelike tongue lolled out of the old man's mouth, wrapping itself around his wife's neck. The dog was staring at him as it furiously humped the old woman's leg.

Vincent ran.

He needed to get as far away from them, from all of this, as he could. He needed to get home, to get his fix. It was called a fix for a reason, as he knew it would fix all of his problems, all of his ills. He just needed to get there safely, and quickly.

A dark, velvety laugh he recognised echoed through the air. He closed his eyes and ran. "*You better run along now*," the disembodied voice mocked him. "*It's getting a little... late, isn't it?*"

He turned.

The silhouette of the dealer was behind him. He was still laughing. His bald head was accentuated in the twilight, his glowing red eyes piercing the near darkness. The couple and their vile dog were close behind him.

As were the two police cars.

They were driving slowly. All he could see of the drivers were shadows, shadows with red eyes and huge, too-wide smiles. He turned again. His house was farther down the road than it had been before. The street looked like it was stretching out before him.

The spaces between him and safety were erupting.

The paving blocks were now swimming on a sea of molten lava. Things were reaching out of the hellish inferno below, grasping and scratching for him, trying to pull him down to dwell with them in their fiery torment for all eternity.

He ran.

He ran with all the strength his weakened body could muster.

The faster he ran, the faster the shadow, the couple with their dog, and the police cars chased him, the faster the *things* beneath him grasped.

Eventually he was at the door. It was within his grasp. As he lunged at it, one of the fiery beasts grabbed him. He could feel his foot burning, the plastic of his cheap boots melting in its grip. It burned his flesh, the agony causing him to scream.

The key was in the lock in a flash, and as the door opened, he fell inside the dingy house. His foot screaming at him, the searing torture making him feel like it was in flames.

He turned and kicked at the door. He caught it and slamming it closed, blocking the grasping beasts, the evil shadow, the vile couple with the dog, and the police.

He was safe now.

He closed his eyes and attempted to refill the depleted breath in his chest. He had no strength in his arms, his back, or his legs.

All he could do was breathe as he lay on back, trying to slow his racing heart.

Eventually, strength seeped back into his extremities, and he reached inside his pocket. His shaking fingers found the small package and wrapped themselves around it. He sighed as he removed it.

He tore the brown paper and held the small plastic bag that was inside in his hand. He allowed his cold fingers to caress it, making the thick red liquid inside squish at his touch.

A tear welled in the corner of his eye as he tore into the blood pack. His stomach growled and twisted as he put it to his mouth, sucking every single drop from it. He ripped the plastic apart and licked every last molecule of blood from every seam of the bag.

When there was nothing left, he dropped the remains and rested his head on the floor. "I'll *never* let it get that bad again," he lied as he felt strength rushing through his body.

He stood, stretched, and looked towards the window.

Vincent pulled the curtains away and peered at the

burgeoning morning. He shielded his eyes from the burn of the sun as it beamed down from between the thin clouds. He watched as the couple walked past his house, their yapping little mutt on his leash.

They looked normal to him; there were no long tongues or inhuman grins. "I'll see you two freaks soon," he whispered. "Your little dog too." He laughed at the obvious film reference. It had been one of his favourites, and he remembered going to see it at the cinema on the day of its release.

He looked down at his foot. The sun catching him as he fell into the house had burnt his flesh, the heat of it eating through his boot. He smiled as he watched the skin melding, knitting itself back on his limb.

He flexed his fingers, revelling in the strength that was back, surging through his body. The taste on the back of his throat was back too.

The metallic tang was nice.

It reminded him of back in the day, when they all used to party all night.

Vincent was nodding almost absently as two police cars passed his window. *Tonight, I'll party again*, he thought. *It'll be just like the old days!*

# Soul Searcher Origins

## Justin Boote

Susanne grunted and rubbed her eyes, slowly opening them and looking around the almost pitch-black room. A sliver of light poked in through a small gap in the curtains, giving her just enough light to see. Enough light so the shadows around the room were not suspicious enough for her to worry about lurking monsters or giant creatures. But something had woken her, and it wasn't her bladder in desperate need of release. Everywhere, both inside and outside, was silent.

Her bedroom door was slightly ajar, a concession made to her cat should it decide to join her for the night, but also in case she saw or heard something that might require her to scream for her parents or make a mad dash to their room if necessary. Susanne often saw or heard things in the middle of the night or when she was just drifting off, yet no matter how many times she swore it was real, her dad also swore it was just a nightmare.

If this was the case, how did nightmares make things in her room move of their own accord? Her mum said she imagined it or probably moved things herself when she got up in the night to go to the toilet, but Susanne didn't think so. In fact, she knew, because she saw them move with her own eyes: a fluttering of pages from one of her schoolbooks; pens rolling off her writing desk when there wasn't a breeze and the window was closed; a slight tug of her blanket.

Dad said now she was getting older—she just turned four—her imagination was growing, too, and when she was asleep, it was sometimes hard to separate dreams from reality. But Susanne knew perfectly well she wasn't dreaming when the shadow in the far corner, its outline a perfect silhouette of a human being, glided across the room towards her. That time she had screamed so loudly, her parents came bursting into the room thinking she fell out of bed and seriously hurt herself. They were quite annoyed when she told them what happened.

It wasn't her fault. She didn't ask to see such things, and it only started happening shortly after her birthday a few weeks ago. The first time, she had been drifting off to sleep, the cat purring beside her, when it suddenly jumped up and hissed at something at the foot of her bed before bolting. Not understanding what was going on, she was about to turn on the lamp beside her when she saw it—a pair of eyes, like twinkling stars, staring right at her. As her own eyes slowly adjusted to the dark, she made out the silhouette of a person crouching, just their head and shoulders in view and long, scraggly hair flowing out behind. The ghostly figure was smiling at Susanne—that much she could tell—but it hadn't made any difference, because Susanne stiffened then screamed for her mum and dad to come and catch the woman in her room. Yet despite making her dad look under the bed and in her wardrobe, the woman disappeared.

That was almost two weeks ago, and the ghostly visitations continued. Sometimes Susanne cowered under the blanket, closing her eyes tightly and wishing the thing to go away; other times she screamed before the woman could touch her with wrinkled, gnarled fingers, always a toothless grin on her old face. And it was because of the darkness in the room, barely able to discern any real features, and also because she was too terrified to take much notice, the connections weren't made until a few nights later.

She had gotten into bed, tired and overly excited after playing all evening, and thoughts of ghosts and strange women in her room were totally forgotten. It was only as she started to fall asleep she noticed a sharp drop in the temperature. Absently pulling the blanket closer to her chin, she was almost asleep when she heard a whisper. Susanne ignored it until she heard it again, slightly louder. Or was it closer? Now awake, the whisper came for a third time, and she could hear it more clearly—her name being whispered softly. As always, tears welled in sleepy eyes. She silently wished for the thing to just go away and leave her alone while at the same time getting ready to scream for her parents should the woman remain. She felt a tug at the blanket, the corner near her shoulder.

"Susy, it's me," said the voice.

There was something familiar yet alien about it, and she couldn't make the connection despite feeling as though she should.

"Hi, Susy. It's me."

The blanket was tugged harder as if the ghost wanted Susanne to open her eyes and see her, but this was the last thing she wanted.

"Go away!" she pleaded.

"But it's me, Susy. You remember me, don't you?"

That voice, soft and gentle, was not as she imagined a terrifying monster at all. Then it occurred to her.

Just a few weeks ago, her grandmother died. Susanne was devasted. Her grandmother, Lily, was her favourite, always telling her funny stories from when she was a little girl. She made the best chocolate sponge cake Susanne ever ate. Susanne went to the funeral with her parents, and she wasn't surprised to see so many people there sobbing and crying. Everyone loved Lily. It was now, lying in bed listening to that voice, she realised why she recognised it.

She dared to pull the blanket down past her eyes slightly and open one of them, a mere squint. The ghost was bending near Susanne's head and smiling. Now that she was up close, she knew who it was.

"Grannie? Is that you?" she whispered.

"Why, yes! Of course it is! Please don't be scared. I'm not here to scare you."

"But...but you're dead. Why are you here again?"

"My body is dead, little Susy, but not my spirit. I just wanted to come and see you again, to say goodbye. I never got the chance before."

"So you're not dead?"

"I know it's hard to understand, but you will, in time. You've been blessed, little one, with a gift. It may not seem like a gift sometimes, but believe me, when you're older, you'll learn to see it as such. You've been blessed with the gift of sight. Now, you be good, listen to your parents, but don't talk to them about this—they won't understand. In time, you'll come to make friends that will help you. Friends that are going to help me right now to move on.

"I love you, little Susy. Maybe we'll see each other again soon."

And with that, Lily slowly faded away.

Susanne never saw her grandmother again, but she did start seeing others. Sometimes, on her way to school, a figure would wave to her from across the street, then when Susanne looked back again, the figure was gone, and too quickly for it to have been a real person. When her mum took her to the park after school, on several occasions she saw a woman standing by herself, crying. When Susanne dared to approach a little closer, she could hear the woman moaning a name, Kristy. Susanne learned the next day a young girl about Susanne's age had fallen from the swings a few months ago and died after banging her head. The mother, crippled with guilt and grief, killed herself just days later.

But Susanne wasn't scared of these apparitions any-more. She understood they weren't here to hurt her, only that she could see them until they finally moved on, just as her grandmother had done. It even made her feel special; she had her own little secret, something only she was privy to. It became quite common for her mother to ask her who she was waving to when there was nobody there. Susanne told her she had a secret friend, and nothing more was said about it.

Tonight, though, things were different.

It had been several days since her grandmother's final visit, and nothing else had occurred in her home since, so she was quite surprised to feel the noticeable drop in temperature, even colder than it usually was in such moments. She had learned not to be scared of any visitations if and when they might appear, as her grandmother had explained. They weren't here to hurt her; they were just lost souls in many cases, or wanting to say one last goodbye to loved ones. Souls searching for closure.

There was a nasty smell this time, too, something that made her eyes sting, like when the cat once brought in a dead mouse and left it hidden behind a piece of furniture. When her dad brought it out and held it in the air, it had been the worst thing she smelled in her life.

The doors to her wardrobe rattled as if something was trying to get out. The pungent odour of rot grew stronger, causing her to gag as she fully awoke.

"Hello? Who is it?" she called. Maybe it was her grandmother again, with another message.

An assortment of crayons and junk on her desk rattled, then one by one flew across the room, all in her direction, narrowly missing her, some of them so hard and fast they exploded upon impact, causing her to gasp. As if a gust of wind suddenly rose, her curtains blew wildly, almost pulled from their railings, the wardrobe doors rattling so hard splinters appeared in the frame.

It occurred to Susanne something was very wrong with all this. This was surely not some poor ghost looking to say hello, and definitely not her grandmother returning. The smell intensified, a combination of rotting vegetables and sulphur. Her bedroom door slowly closed, as if guided by an invisible hand, while at the same time, the doors to her wardrobe creaked open then slammed against the wall, causing plaster to crack in places.

Susanne opened her mouth to scream, but as though someone clamped a hand over her mouth, nothing came out. She tried to jump out of bed and run to her parents, asleep in their own bed, but she was frozen, her legs failing to move, a great weight pushing down on her, sucking the oxygen from her lungs.

Movement came from inside the wardrobe, her clothes hanging from the pole brushed aside leaving a great, dark space. In that space, two glowing eyes appeared, like flames flickering, alternating colours from orange to bright red. The whole wardrobe shook as if someone was standing behind it and rattling it as hard as they could.

A hand appeared, gripping the side of the frame. It had long, gnarled, black fingers, fingernails like the bears she once saw at the zoo, abnormally long and sharp. They clicked on the wooden frame for a few seconds, then one finger pointed in her direction and beckoned her as though daring her to meet whatever lurked inside.

A warmth beneath her told her she had wet herself, but she was barely aware.

From the entrance to the wardrobe, an elongated shadow grew, darker than the dark itself, visible despite the only source of light being the moon shining through her window. It continued growing until it reached the side of her bed where her pillow lay, clearly the shape of a head but impossibly wide. Those burning orbs were in the shadow as well, looking up at her.

As Susanne continued staring, unable to take her eyes off it as though forced to watch, the shadow took on a more substantiated form as though being inflated. It rose, like a person lying on the floor being lifted up, until finally the top of its head bumped against the ceiling. A deep, resonating cackle bounced around the room. Its body appeared to have multiple arms swinging behind it like an octopus, waving around as though underwater. It looked down at Susanne and pointed at her with all its limbs while a huge, cavernous mouth opened revealing teeth that should have been too long to fit in its mouth.

"Stay away," it said, its voice a crack of lightning, almost bursting Susanne's eardrums.

"Their souls are mine."

It launched itself at her, its massive body about to squash her flat until, at the last second, too fast for Susanne to even compute what was happening, it disappeared, leaving the room in complete silence once again.

Minutes or hours seemed to pass as Susanne lay there, in and out of consciousness, until eventually she seemed to come to. As though in a daze, she slowly pushed herself up and swung her legs over the side of the bed, and headed to her parent's bedroom, crawling into their bed and snuggling up beside her sleeping father and instantly falling asleep herself. The next morning, her parents asked her what happened for her to come to their room, but she simply shook her head and shrugged, saying she couldn't remember.

But that night, as she lay in bed, terrified the creature may appear once more, four shadowy figures materialised in front of her, smiles on their semi-transparent faces.

*Don't be scared*, they all said in unison yet their mouths tightly closed.

*You don't have to be scared of us. We're here to help.*

"Are you ghosts?"

*Sort of. You could say we're helpers or guides. We search for lost souls and help them move on to their final resting place.*

"Like with my grandma?"

*Exactly.*

"So you're soul searchers, then!"

*Yes! We'll be seeing you soon, little Susy. Very soon!*

# Eat Me

## Caitlin Marceau

*Previously Published in* Dethfest Confessions: The Devil's Playlist, *December 2023*

I wave goodbye to the audience crowded around Stage 2 and dramatically blow kisses to them with both my hands. I wink and smile at whoever catches my eye, making sure to play into my flirty persona, before following my bandmates off stage.

"That was bullshit, and you fucking know it," I hiss under my breath once I'm sure the sound technicians have turned the microphones off and there's no risk of the crowd hearing me.

"It *was* bullshit, Shiloh. It's why we fucking cut you off," Salem whispers back at me, absentmindedly combing his beard down with his hand.

I shake my head and push past him, annoyed, making my way to the metal stairs leading us away from the stage. We walk silently through the scorching sun and tall grass to where the band trailers are parked, waving to fans who manage to catch a glimpse of us from behind the barricades and privacy fences. My leather pants and skimpy lace corset feel uncomfortably tight in the summer heat, and even my normally-comfortable Doc Martens are too warm for me to bear. Hair sticks to the back of my sweat-streaked neck, and I try not to think about how much my makeup has smudged down my face since starting our set.

I see our trailer in the distance—a banner with Sexxx written across it hangs off the side of the metal monstrosity in intentionally-campy blood-red cursive-and-black detailing—and sigh with relief. I spot one of the Dethfest volunteers waiting outside of it with bottles of water glistening with condensation and nod my thanks as I grab two out of their hands, making my way into the cramped space.

I sit on the edge of my small cot and toss one of the bottles next to me on the thin mattress, cracking the other one open and chugging most of the water. I breathe deeply, gulping in air, before slamming the last of it back. Halfway through untying my boots, the rest of the band filters in.

"We need to talk about what happened," Moss, our drummer, says quietly. Despite her ferocious way around a drum set and the extroverted personality she puts on for our shows, the woman is generally soft-spoken and even a little timid. For as long as I've known her, she has avoided conflict like the plague, so for her to suggest we talk about the show means things are getting serious.

"Yeah, we do," I say, kicking my shoes off and standing up beside my bed. I pull the duffle bag out from underneath it and make my way to the bathroom in the back of the trailer. I slam the door closed behind me and begin to wash up, eager to get free of my restrictive costume and feel clean again.

"That was a real dick move of you to put us in that spot, Shiloh," Salem yells through the bathroom door. "We told you that we didn't want to play that song."

I zip the fly closed on my jean shorts, pull my baggy black T-shirt over my head, and open the bathroom door.

"Then it's a good thing you didn't have to! You didn't even let me get through the fucking chorus!" I spit, annoyed.

Pushing past him, I throw my duffle back under my bed and sit on top of the small cot, pulling on fresh socks and slipping my feet into a pair of worn Converse.

"Because none of us were comfortable with it!" he shouts.

Moss and Piper, our bassists, sit together quietly on one of the long benches at the front by the door. Although they don't nod in agreement with Salem, they're not quick to speak out against him, either, and he continues to yell at me.

"We've told you a thousand fucking times that we're not comfortable with the shit you've been writing! We don't play music about eating people and brutally torturing them! We play music about falling in love and getting railed!" He holds up his hands in frustration, chewing me out. "But you just *had* to perform that song anyway!"

"You guys try new fucking material all the goddamned

time, but the second I do it, you—"

"When we try something new, generally the rest of the band is in on it! Or we're just doing a quick riff during our introductions! We don't just start playing a random song in the middle of our set." Piper frowns, crossing her arms in front of her chest. "That song was gross, Shiloh."

"That song was *great*," I snap.

"It was freaking me out, and it was freaking the crowd out too," Moss says under her breath.

"Bullshit! They were into it, and you know it! You're such a liar, you little—"

"Stop arguing, Shiloh!" Salem's voice reverberates off the walls, reminding us all why he's the lead singer. "If we've told you once, we've told you a thousand times: we don't want to play whatever the fuck *that* was."

"You guys didn't even give it a chance."

"And we don't have to! We're Sexxx! We're all about flirting and fun and pop metal! We get people horny and give them a fun show! That's it! That's the schtick!"

"Maybe I want more than that!" I scream at them.

"Then maybe you need to find another band!" Salem shouts back at me.

I wait for Piper or Moss to speak up, to tell Salem he's out of line this time, but that moment never comes. Neither dares to meet my gaze, to look me in the eye, while I stare at them.

"Seriously?" I finally ask, voice barely above a whisper.

He sighs and leans against the wall of the trailer, running a hand through his sweaty hair. Salem finally shrugs and looks at me, silent, before eventually finding the words.

"If you can't get on board with our sound and what we want, and if you keep pushing this heavier fucked-up shit on us, then yeah. You should find another band."

"And who the fuck is going to write most of your music for you? Who's going to put up with your shit, you talentless hacks?" I ask, failing to keep the fury out of my voice.

"Don't you fucking call us—"

"*We* aren't Sexxx. *I* am! This was *my* idea. These are *my* songs. This is *my* band. And if you don't like the direction *I'm* taking us in, then *you* can leave!"

"It *was* your band," Moss says quietly, "but it's bigger than just you now."

"*We're* bigger than you now," Piper adds, pursing her lips together and finally looking me in the eyes.

"If you want to find new musicians and call yourselves Sexxx, then go for it. We won't stop you. But if you think for even a second that using our name and writing the same mediocre shit that you've been writing for years makes *you* this band, then you're as dumb as the bimbo you play on stage." Salem crosses the trailer and looms over where I'm sitting. He looks down at me, his eyes as icy as his voice. "We've outgrown you, Shiloh. We've known this for a long time. We just were too kind to admit it. So, get your shit together or get the fuck out."

I stand up, my body pressed against him, and hold his gaze. Even with him towering over me, I refuse to cower away from Salem or give an inch. I square my shoulders and stick my chest out, glaring up at him.

"Get out of my way," I say, seething with rage.

He opens his mouth like he's going to argue about this too, but eventually, he closes his lips and stands aside. I push past him, making sure to slam my shoulder into his torso when I squeeze by, and make my way to the trailer door, throwing it open and storming out.

Snippets of a hushed conversation follow as the three of them discuss me.

"What crawled up...and died?" Piper asks.

"I...how she treated...us," Moss whispers to them.

"...just needs a good...'uck is all." Salem laughs.

I storm through the tall grass, passing rows of trailers, heading to the hidden festival entrance for the bands. One of the security guards spots me approaching the metal barricade and stands up a little straighter. He opens his mouth, and I shake my head at him, hoping to kill off any conversation before it can begin. As much as I normally try to make polite conversation with the people working at these events, I don't have the energy right now, and I want to avoid drawing unnecessary attention to myself.

Without my stage makeup and tight corset, it can be easy to pass by crowds of people without them immediately recognizing me. But if I'm spotted talking with security on this side of the restricted entrance, what little cover I have will be blown.

I keep my head down and pass by the guard, following the trail cut into the dirt and grass by what seems like a million festivalgoers. Another volunteer is passing out bottles of water to the crowd, and I grab another one, still thirsty despite slamming back two of them already. I twist the cap off and drink. Some of the cold water spills over my lips and down my neck, sending a shiver through me.

I walk past a few stalls selling merch, most from bands

I know and some from bands I don't, and feel myself turning red when I spot the booth selling T-shirts and hoodies with Sexxx and our photo silkscreened across the front of them. At first, I think I'm blushing with embarrassment at seeing myself plastered across the stall, but I quickly realize my hands are balled into fists and my jaw is clenched. I'm not red because I'm mortified; I'm red with fury at being betrayed by the band.

At being betrayed by *my* band.

"Over my dead body," I mumble.

Someone near the Sexxx booth looks my way. I wonder if I'm just being paranoid about them recognizing me, but when they jab their friend in the ribs with an elbow and nod their head in my direction, I know I've been made. Not wanting to get mobbed by a pack of fans, I turn on my heels and quickly put as much distance between myself and the booth as I can.

The hot summer air smells like smoke, sweat, and stale beer. As I walk around the grounds of the venue, weaving through the horde of festivalgoers, my stomach starts to growl. I realize I haven't had anything to eat since early that morning. I debate going back to the trailer for free food, but knowing that means having to face my bandmates, I resign myself to the painfully long wait in one of the food tent queues.

I get in line and cross my arms in front of my chest, trying to calm myself down from the rage I've been in since—

I stop and think about it.

I've been mad since my song was cut off during the concert, but I know that's not when this anger started. I want to convince myself the feeling started a few months ago when they told me they were unhappy with the direction I was trying to take the band in, but that's a lie too. The truth is I've been angry for a long time. This quiet rage has been building inside me for years—maybe since birth—but I've been so busy channelling it into my music that I never noticed how big it's gotten or how it threatens to devour me whole.

*We've outgrown you, Shiloh.*

I picture Salem's face, and another wave of anger rolls through me. I breathe heavily, remembering the way his eyes twinkled with malice, the smug smile he tried to hide while threatening everything I worked for, and the way he stood over me, trying to make me feel small. The memory of him makes me seethe, and I wonder if he coerced, bullied, or manipulated Piper and Moss into seeing things his way.

God knows it wouldn't be the first time if he had.

My flushed skin feels too hot and too tight, and I pull at the neck of my T-shirt, fanning myself with the soft cotton in an attempt to find some relief as I wait for my turn at the food tent. The sun overhead is unforgiving, and it doesn't help to improve my bad mood. My stomach growls again, louder this time, and the smell of barbecued hotdogs and hamburgers has my mouth watering. Normally I'm not a fan of the scent, but right now, I can't get enough of it.

The man in line ahead of me runs a hand through his thick black hair, the long waves tumbling down his back. They're gorgeous in the bright sun, and I'm tempted to reach out and touch them. As if he hears me, he begins to gather his hair together at the nape of his neck, accidentally swatting me with it as he pulls it through the loop of his elastic, tying it up into a ponytail. He turns around and smiles at me, his honey-brown eyes pushing away the memory of Salem's cold blue ones.

"Sorry about that."

"No worries," I tell him, too busy admiring his full lips to remember I should smile back.

He starts turning back but stops. His brows come together, and he studies my face. After a second, his eyes widen in recognition and he smiles excitedly.

"No way! You're the guitarist for Sexxx! Shiloh, right?"

I open my mouth, ready to deny the claim. People within earshot begin to buzz with excitement, while he continues talking.

"That song you were playing—the one during the intro thing you guys do—was fucking amazing! *So* hardcore. I loved it!"

I smile wide, my heart beating wildly and my skin getting even warmer with excitement as I look at the man. "You liked my song?"

The buzzing and whispering around me gets louder. A few of the people from the line leave their spots to crowd around me, each trying to get a view of my face to make sure I am who the man says I am.

"I fucking *loved* it!"

I take a step toward him, excited, my stomach growling loud and long when I catch a whiff of the man's sweat on his skin. It blends in with the smell of the meats wafting from the food vendors.

"Really?"

More people gather around us. Their bodies are warm, and between the heat radiating off of them and the sun, it's unbearable. I pull at my T-shirt again, suddenly hyper-aware of how the clothing rubs against my body and sticks to my sweat-dampened skin.

The man must feel similarly. He wipes perspiration from his forehead with the back of his hand and pulls at the front of his shirt. I lick my lips and look at him, catching a glimpse of his stomach and hips when his T-shirt rides up a bit.

My stomach growls again.

"Fuck yes." His eyes are wide and unfocused as he looks at me. "It was unlike anything I've heard from you guys. I mean, not that I don't like your other stuff, but this...This was intense. Visceral."

I nod my head violently in agreement.

The people around us move closer. Their sweat, their breath, their skin, their blood—all of it mixes with the thick smoke from the grills inside the tent. I breathe deeply, enjoying the scent instead of being repulsed by it.

"That's what I wanted," I whisper excitedly, pulling hard at the collar of my T-shirt, the cotton ripping. "I wanted something raw and brutal."

"That line about peeling back flesh and devouring demons..." he trails off, standing even closer as his eyes take in my body. "It really made sense to me," he finally finishes.

Heat rolls off of his skin, and I feel dizzy, drinking in the smell of the man, placing a hand on my stomach that aches and groans with hunger, swallowing saliva as my mouth waters.

"I think that's because we're all hungry for something—acceptance, love, validation, whatever—and the only way for us to get it is if we're willing to consume the part of us, the demon, that's holding us back." I'm not entirely sure what I'm saying or that I believe any of the bullshit spilling from my lips. What I *am* certain of is the desperation growing inside me with each passing second.

"I wish you could have finished playing your song," the man says, his breath hot on my face.

"So do I."

My clothes feel so hot against my skin that for a second, I think they might be burning me. My stomach bellows, ravenous, and my body bristles with tension from both my earlier confrontation with Salem and the energy currently pulsing between myself and this stranger. My muscles are tense and feel like they're going to snap, like I've been coiled too tight.

The air is thick, and at first, I think it's so solid and heavy that it's pushing me around, making me rock on my feet. But when I look closer, I realize it's not the air moving me, but rather, it's the mass of bodies crowded around me, swaying and heaving together as one.

I stare at the man, his honey-brown eyes locking onto my own, and the movement of the crowd gets faster. It's hard to breathe, the air is like fire in my lungs, and soon, all of us are holding our breaths. The swaying gradually slows, and everyone comes to a stop, the world around us silent.

And then: chaos.

The crowd explodes into a frenzy.

They grab at each other, ripping their clothes off and fitting their bodies together however they can. All thoughts of modesty and decency are gone, erupting into a fury of flesh and desire.

I throw myself at the man, clawing at his shirt. I tear it off of him and drop it in the dirt beside us before running my hands up his chest, my fingers tracing the firm muscles and soft curves of his body. He rips my shirt off, too, and unhooks my bra, kissing a trail from my mouth to my chest, his lips finding my nipples. I sigh, letting my head roll back on my shoulders, and let out a loud moan when I feel his teeth pierce into me, biting off a small piece of my right breast.

It should hurt—on some level, I'm sure it does—but it sends a quiver of ecstasy through me. I grab a fistful of the man's hair, enjoying the way his smooth locks feel between my callused fingers, and guide his lips back up to mine. I kiss him deeply, delighting in the taste of myself on his lips, and I savour the way my warm blood runs down my chest, over my stomach, and drips onto my thighs.

He pulls his mouth away from mine and continues to chew the piece of my breast. I take one of his hands in my own and lead it to my mouth, kissing his palm. Slipping his index and middle finger past my lips, I suck on his skin before sinking my teeth into them. I chew carefully, not wanting to bite through the bone, and slowly begin stripping his fingers of their meat.

The man moans and pulls me closer to him, grinding himself against me. He lowers his head and takes another bite, this time out of my shoulder. Someone presses themselves against me, and I shiver in delight as they roam my body, their sharp nails leaving deep cuts that bloom red in their wake.

Once I've cleaned the sinew from the man's two fingers, I guide his hand down, past the waistband of both my shorts and underwear, and between my legs. I pant softly, using him to rub myself, enjoying the sensation of the hard bones and hot blood against the softness of my body. Pressure begins to build and grow deep inside me, and my pulse thunders in my veins.

When I feel like I can't take anymore, I slip his skinned fingers inside me and thrust against them. Soon, my eyes roll back in my head and my legs shake as I feel more teeth pulling at my skin. A wave of pleasure rushes through me, and I cry out in release, my mouth finding someone else's. We share a sloppy kiss, and they push the flesh they were chewing into my mouth with their tongue.

The man withdraws his hand and turns his attention to a woman next to him. She's covered in blood and missing her nose, but nobody seems to care. They begin to gyrate against each other, while another set of hands guides me deeper into the crowd.

As good as I feel, as right as I feel, there's still something missing. I'm still not whole.

I'm not *sated*.

I let myself get swept up in the fervour of the crowd, enjoying the way our bodies become one body. I see a pair of blue eyes watching me.

For a second, I think it's Salem, but when I blink, his face disappears just as quickly as I imagined it. Someone's hands dig inside me, working me open and pulling me apart. As I let myself quake with pleasure, I know what I have to do.

The air that's been hot on my skin all day finally feels cold, and I can't help but shiver as I approach the trailer. Although a light is on, nothing but silence emanates from inside the space. I slowly climb the small steps and grab the cold metal handle, pulling open the stiff door. Ambling inside, I look around, noticing both Piper and Moss aren't here.

Salem, on the other hand, sits on a nearby couch, lazily flipping through the pages of a book. After a minute of pretending not to notice my arrival, he finally looks up at me, and his bored expression turns to one of shock and confusion.

"Oh my God, Shiloh, what the fuck happened to you?" he shouts. He looks me up and down, his eyes finding all the places my skin should be but isn't. His gaze lingers on my naked breasts, and although he seems genuinely concerned for me, he can't help but stare between my legs at my exposed body.

"I want you inside of me."

"What?" he asks, practically choking out the words.

"I want you inside of me," I say again, crossing the space between us to straddle his lap.

"Shiloh, you're covered in blood and seriously injured. I think you're in shock. We need to get you to a hospit—"

I lean in and kiss him, grinding down on his lap, my lips pressing hard against his. At first, he keeps his mouth closed, resisting me. But soon, his hands are cupping the backs of my thighs, and his lips are pushing back against mine. I keep my eyes open as we kiss, savouring the look of confusion and arousal on his face. I smile to myself—knowing that I'll get what I want—and deepen the kiss, coaxing his lips open with my tongue.

Behind me, the door to the trailer opens, and Piper and Moss talk in panicked voices about the chaos outside. They mention something about the water, but I don't care.

I'm hungry, and only one thing will satiate me.

I continue to tease Salem and feel a rush of joy when he slips his tongue into my mouth.

*Finally.*

I bite down, moaning softly when my teeth crunch through his tongue. He starts to scream and tries to pull away, but that only helps me rip through his flesh and sever the tongue from his mouth. I don't bother chewing the tough muscle. Instead, I let the warm blood coat the back of my throat and swallow it whole.

Salem tries to push me off of him, his arms flailing wildly as he panics. His screams mix in with those of Moss and Piper.

I smile down at him.

"I've outgrown you, Salem," I whisper coldly, and take another bite.

# Playing the Odds

## Jeff Strand

"Fold," said Allen, tossing down his cards. And that was it. He had blown through his gambling budget on the first day. Today was the third day, and he maxed out his credit cards to the tune of $22,000.

He and Kim came to Vegas for their five-year anniversary. He faked a stomach bug this morning by rushing into the bathroom and sticking his finger down his throat and promised her it was okay if she took the bus trip to the Grand Canyon without him. After she left, he spent ten minutes in bed trying to convince himself this was a horrifically bad idea, then went downstairs for an epic poker losing streak.

He stood up, bracing himself against the table to keep from passing out, then walked away.

He had absolutely no idea how Kim would react. Would she sob? Scream? Go deadly quiet? Hand him a revolver and order him to shove it in his mouth? He truly didn't know, although he supposed he would find out later today, unless he hurled himself off the top of the hotel first.

"You okay?" somebody said to him.

Allen glanced over. It was a man, perhaps in his late twenties, wearing a dark blue suit. "Not really, no."

"Would you like to talk about it?"

"Hell no."

"I can fix your problem."

"Oh, really? You're going to pay off my debt?"

"Perhaps."

Allen couldn't help but chuckle. "Well, shit, that's a great big frickin' load off my mind. Everything is just perfect now. What kind of interest rate are you offering? Ninety percent?"

"No interest," said the man. "It's not a loan. It's a game."

"What kind of game?"

The man smiled and extended his hand. "My name's Rick Murray. I'm play-testing a game that could recoup all of your losses ten minutes from now. No financial risk to you whatsoever. You will not lose another penny. Maybe I misinterpreted your facial expression and body language, but you look like somebody who is truly desperate. Am I wrong?"

"No, you figured that shit out perfectly."

"Then come with me."

"Where?"

"My office."

Allen shrugged. "Screw it. Why not? If you're luring me somewhere to kill me, you'll have saved me the trouble of doing it myself."

"Perfect. Follow me."

They left the casino together. Allen followed the other man, not speaking, as they walked to another building. They went inside, where Rick led him across the lobby and into a small office. It didn't look like the kind of place where any games were played. Allen wondered if Rick was going to offer to do his taxes.

Rick started to pull the door shut, then left it open. "Don't want you to feel uncomfortable," he said, sitting down behind the desk, which was mostly empty except for a computer. "Have a seat."

Allen sat down on the chair in front of the desk.

"Can I get you anything?" Rick asked. "Water? Coffee?"

"Whiskey?"

"No alcohol, sorry."

"Then nothing."

"May I ask your name?"

"Allen."

"Last name?"

"Fucked. Allen Fucked."

Rick smiled. "Pleased to meet you, Allen. I'll get right to it. I'm inviting you to participate in a game. After each round, you can decide if you want to keep going or if you want to quit. If you quit, you get to keep your winnings. If you continue, the prizes get bigger and bigger. Now, I need you to be frank with me. How much money have you lost today?"

"I couldn't give you an exact number. I just kept withdrawing cash until my credit cards stopped working."

"Then give me an approximate number."

"Twenty-two, twenty-three. Thousand, not hundred."

"And you don't have that much stuck between the

couch cushions, do you? The loss hurts. I see that you're wearing a wedding band. How will your spouse take the news?"

"Your guess is as good as mine. I don't think she'll give me a reassuring hug."

"Newlyweds?"

"I wish. We were here to celebrate our five-year anniversary."

"Any kids?"

"No, thank God."

Rick nodded. "Let's call your losses twenty-three thousand dollars. What if I told you that I could offer you a 99% chance of winning that money back?"

"I'd say you were full of shit and trying to scam me."

"Fair enough. I wouldn't believe me, either. But that's exactly what I'm offering. In the first round of this game, you'll spin a wheel with one hundred numbers on it. If it lands on the numbers one through ninety-nine, I will immediately deposit twenty-five thousand dollars into your bank account or, if you prefer, hand you an envelope full of cash. All your anguish is erased, just like that. You'll walk out of here a new man. Ninety-nine percent chance. Forgive my unprofessional language, but those are pretty fucking good odds."

"And what if, for the sake of argument, I don't land on the numbers one through ninety-nine?"

"We break your arm."

"You do what?"

"We break your arm. Like I said, there's no financial risk on your part, but yes, if you spin the wheel and it lands on the number zero, we will break your arm."

"What's the catch?" asked Allen.

Rick frowned. "I believe I just told you."

"No, there's got to be something more than that. No way are you giving me a 99% percent chance of winning the money. It's totally rigged."

Rick stood up. "Let's go into the game room."

They left Rick's office and went into the room next door, which wasn't much bigger than the office. A brightly colored wheel, maybe three feet in diameter, was mounted on the far wall. Next to it was a chair with a weird-ass contraption on the armrest.

"That's our wheel," said Rick. "One hundred possible numbers. The one you don't want is zero, which you can see is dark red on a black background. The designer wanted to add a skull, but we overruled him. You spin the wheel. Anything but zero and you're instantly twenty-five thousand dollars richer."

"No way. That's too easy. This has to be a scam."

"You mean we enhanced it with a magnet or something?"

"Yeah."

"I'm told that every single player we've brought in here has asked that. And the answer is: it's not, but we can't prove it. So we can make whatever accommodations you want. You can roll a pair of ten-sided dice. You can write the numbers zero through ninety-nine on slips of paper and draw one out of a hat. Any fair way you can think of to generate a random number, we can work with. We're not here to con you. I promise, you will have a 99% chance of winning the money."

"Fine," said Allen. "What do I have to lose? Let's do this shit."

"Before you officially commit, I'll explain how the

chair works. You'll sit down and place your left arm in the armrest. In the extremely unlikely event that you lose, I'll press a button and that very heavy iron block will slam down onto your arm, hitting it right below the elbow. It will smash your forearm into that deep groove in the armrest, breaking it in at least two places."

"Oh," said Allen. "Oh, wow. That ain't right."

"It's not a hairline fracture. Your arm will be *broken*."

"Hey, Kim might do worse to me. She'll probably break my damn neck."

"Do you feel like you have all the information necessary to make your decision?"

"Yeah."

"Then I hate to do this to you, but it *is* a game, right? The offer expires in sixty seconds."

"How many times do I have to say it? Let's do this."

"Glad to hear it," said Rick. "Looks like it's time for you to win some money. Have a seat."

Allen plopped down into the chair.

Rick crouched down beside the chair and fastened some Velcro straps over Allen's wrist. "Is that to make sure I don't try to escape?" asked Allen.

"Yes, sir."

"You don't have anything to worry about. If I don't win my money back, I'll probably shove my head in there."

Rick smiled. "Spin the wheel. We use *Price is Right* rules—it must go all the way around at least once. Good luck to you."

"Thanks." Allen reached out with his free hand and gave the wheel a spin.

It went all the way around a couple of times.

Finally landing on...

Zero.

Allen and Rick both stared at the motionless wheel.

"Fuck," said Allen.

"Hold on," said Rick. "That's never happened before."

"The wheel is rigged. Admit it."

"No, the wheel is most definitely not rigged. The game is completely fair. I guess it was bound to happen at some point—a one-percent chance isn't much of a chance, but it's still a chance. If we run the game a hundred times, the odds are that it's going to happen at least once. I just wasn't expecting it."

"Me, either," said Allen. "Obviously."

"Here's the thing. This was just the first step in a much more elaborate game. You were going to get through this one, and then I was going to offer you even more money to play a game with slightly worse odds. It was going to be this ongoing series of challenges where the prizes kept increasing but the tasks grew more and more difficult. And you'd soon learn that you were trapped in the game with no way to escape." Rick let out a long, deep sigh. "Damn it."

"I'm happy to play a game like that," said Allen. "Bring on the ongoing series of challenges. I'm ready."

"I can't. The integrity of this whole enterprise is at stake. It just seems like a waste to have found an excellent candidate and then get rid of him before we've done anything."

"I'll spin the wheel again, no problem."

"That's not how the game works."

"We could pretend it didn't go all the way around."

"I need to make a quick call," said Rick, taking out his cell phone. "Hi, it's me. You saw what happened, right? Do you think there's any way we could... No, no, I totally understand. Nothing is more important than the integrity of the game. I thought he'd be a fun player, but you're absolutely right. Thank you." He disconnected the call and shoved his cell phone back into his pocket. "All right, Mr. Fucked, you spun the wheel, and now you must face the consequences of losing."

Rick pressed the button. The iron block dropped, smashing Allen's arm into the groove. He shrieked in pain as three different shards of broken bone burst through the skin.

"I'm very sorry about this," said Rick, tearing open the Velcro straps and speaking loudly to be heard over Allen's screams. "We do have a medical team, so we'll get your arm fixed up as much as possible."

"You fucking psychopath!" Allen wailed.

"There's no reason to be impolite. You did know the rules before you agreed to participate."

Allen stood up, then fell to his knees, sobbing.

"Look at the bright side," said Rick. "Your injuries might earn your wife's sympathy. She could be more inclined to forgive you for the financial loss."

"Did I lose?" Allen asked.

"Obviously. Look at your mangled limb."

"I mean, am I *out?*"

Rick frowned. "Are you saying you wish to keep going?"

Allen nodded.

"I'm not certain you're in the best state of mind right now."

"Let's do it! What's the next game?"

"Same game as before, actually, but with a larger prize

and greater odds that your arm will be broken."

"Can I use the same arm?"

"No."

Allen stood back up and plopped onto the seat. "Fuck it. Let's do it."

# Attached

## Ben Young

From: *Voices in the Dark, Paranormal Phenomena Explained* by Katherine Guterman (pg. 56)

"Inhuman Spirits":

These are similar to other *Intelligent Spirits* (see pg. 22) in that they can have intelligent interactions with the living and that they exhibit consistent traits such as appearance, habits, biases, smells, etc. They are also aware of what is happening in the present—as opposed to *Residual Spirits* (see pg. 14)—and will indicate responses or reactions to events as they happen, particularly with change.

However, a distinct difference from the previous entries here is the complete lack of any prior human existence. Put plainly, inhuman spirits are those spirits that were *never* human, and they likely were never "alive" in any manner we would understand. This can lead us to apply a variety of terms with religious connotations (most commonly angels and demons), but I would argue terms like that are subjective and limited in their meaning. The names applied to inhuman spirits vary greatly, yet their descriptions hold much commonality. In most reported cases, these spirits act to deceive the living by taking on human forms, including the impersonation of loved ones or other trusted persons. However, when an inhuman spirit attempts to appear human, they invariably fall short because they have never truly been human. Humanity remains foreign to them, causing their projection of it to be incomplete. This typically results in some slight visual distortion in one or more parts of their mimicked form.

From my studies, there seems to be a correlation between the level of a person's psychic sensitivity and the appearance of inhuman spirits. While it is difficult to find any concrete evidence or proof, it seems reasonable to say that those of us gifted with ESP or other enhanced mental capabilities are more likely to encounter spirits. It is also possible that an extremely strong mind can act as a beacon for this specific type of spirit, even attracting them in some cases. When this happens, there is a far greater chance of the spirit becoming *Attached* (see pg. 80).

I want to state very clearly that contact with inhuman spirits is inherently dangerous. There is too much we do not—and *cannot*—know about them, their abilities, and their intentions. My advice, should you encounter an inhuman spirit, is simple. Be extremely cautious. Avoid interaction by any means possible, even if you believe its intentions to be benevolent. Do not respond to questions or share any information, thoughts, or feelings with it. Any knowledge it acquires can be used to manipulate you. Most importantly, avoid doing or saying anything that would give it permission to engage with you or enter your space. I have heard numerous cases of fairly harmless interactions escalating into something dangerous immediately after permission was given to the spirit. This is usually where attachment begins.

If a spirit is attempting to reach you and you are unable to break contact, seek help from an experienced medium immediately. Once these entities become attached to a living person, they can follow anywhere that person goes with ease, and it is very difficult and perilous to remove them.

Make no mistake, an inhuman spirit with malicious intent will take great effort to deceive you and to obtain what it desires. And they seek only one thing: the destruction of human life.

"Does that look like a face to you?" Lucy Claremont asked. Her gut clenched at the idea of seeing it again. Half the reason she agreed to come here was to escape it.

"Where?" Meredith answered.

Lucy pointed. "Over there, on that wall."

Meredith shook her head. "I don't see anything."

Lucy kept her gaze fixed, but the more she strained to

focus on it, the less sure she felt. A few seconds ago, she was certain of its presence mingled into the woodgrain in that dark corner of the restaurant. A long, drawn-out face with distinctly feminine features. Almost too feminine, if that was a thing a face could be. Exaggerated. High cheekbones and strong angles, but stretched to a near-equine degree. The mouth a bit too petite. The ears sharper than natural.

As they were led to their table, she scanned the room, admiring the austere décor, glad to be out of the house, and met the startling sensation of direct eye contact without seeing a person. A defensive flash went through her lizard brain, and her heart quickened for a few beats. Then she blinked, and it looked like just a coincidental pattern in the wood. But for that one instant...

This wasn't the first time she thought she saw that face, but it was the most distinct. Like it was... stronger.

"You feeling okay?" Meredith asked.

Around them, dishware clinked, low conversations continued, and piped-in jazz music played.

A brief pause lingered as Lucy stared, blinking hard. "I'm fine. Yeah, I'm fine."

Meredith wrinkled her brow, judging the words. "We can go whenever. I mean, I know you weren't eager to come out just yet, and I was a bit pushy. But if this isn't helping you, then, like... we can just go."

They had only known each other for a matter of weeks, but Lucy thought now about the fast kinship she felt with Meredith upon meeting her in a support group for mothers who had lost a child. Their similar experiences went even deeper than that, so the chemistry was instant and their bond erupted. Meredith Livingston was her age, had lived her whole life one county over from Hallstown, and had worked as a nurse in a burn unit before her infant son had died from Sudden Infant Death Syndrome. All her major intersections in life were similar to Lucy's own. Nothing was identical, but it was all... adjacent. It felt like she was Lucy, just two inches to the right or a half day later. They were one another's shadow. Contrasting this, Meredith couldn't do the... things... Lucy could do to reach patients, but most of Meredith's patients were more aware than Lucy's, so it didn't stop her from helping them in tremendous ways. Meredith was a natural caregiver, a pillar of empathy and patience. Just like Lucy.

"No," Lucy said. "You were right. This was a good idea. It's time for me to have some fun again. Come on, I'm fine. Let's have dinner. I'm fine."

"That's four times you said I'm fine, you know?"

"Was it?"

"Mm-hmm. Gets less convincing each time you repeat it."

"Okay, okay. You made your point."

"Maybe just tell me what's on your mind. Let it out, and then we'll see if it's a good idea to stay. It's important for us to get back out into the world, but it's more important that we do it the right way. You're still... *we're* still healing. Talk to me."

That request caused a conflict. Should she tell Meredith about the face she had been seeing? Would it help? Here was a person Lucy had met only recently, yet they knew more about one another than practically anyone else on the planet did. They had cried together a dozen times, shared their deepest darkest, reached out in moments of weakness and panic. Yet there were still massive things Lucy hadn't spoken of. Still secrets.

No. She couldn't say it. Lucy hadn't mentioned seeing that face the last few times and didn't feel comfortable talking about it now. Not because Meredith would call her nuts or think poorly of her. But why, then? There was some other reason, something compelling her not to make Meredith aware she thought an inhuman face was watching her from shadows. She wanted to protect her friend from whatever it might be or whatever it wanted. Lucy decided it was best to keep that little secret, for now at least. It was tiny compared to the other things she wasn't ready to talk about.

Meredith knew about John Camden, about Lucy's experience with him and what it had done for her. But Meredith had no idea what really happened because Lucy didn't talk about her... abilities.

Lucy looked at the dark corner again, scanning for the face, hoping not to see it. Meredith's eyes followed.

Then the server approached and broke her concentration, mercifully.

"Good evening," he said.

And from there, it mostly was.

Lucy enjoyed the night out so much that when she arrived home, she wasn't thinking about the face at all. After dinner, they went to a movie, something neither of them had done in years. The chairs were far more plush than Lucy remembered, and they reclined at the push of a button. The movie was a forgettable romantic comedy with a bland title, but it was lighthearted and quite fun.

But the face was waiting inside her house, and she quickly noticed it was more defined each time she saw it. This time she could even make out its dark, flowing hair as it emerged from a shadow in her unlit front hallway, almost melting into the drywall like fast-growing mold. A phantom, fungal house guest awaiting her return.

Its spectral contours conveyed a deep anguish, like it was in long-standing pain or straining terribly just to be seen. Its eyes burned with life, or something approximate.

Lucy's blood froze.

It was late, near midnight, a time that empowered the whispering fears, when the clarity and surety of the world felt distant, flimsy. Part of her knew this, recognized it even as she locked herself in place, seeing that face down the hall and measuring her breaths until the cloud of terror began to clear. Beneath the fleeting reaction of terror, she wondered if this was another lost soul. Someone she, and only she, could help. Could it be reaching out to her in desperate need?

"I... I'm here," she said, and stepped toward it. "I see you."

The face faded, gone. Lucy walked closer, fighting the urge to turn on the hall light and banish it while she had the chance.

It came back, now so clear, and she was so close it might have been emerging from the wall's surface into three dimensions. It made a soft wailing noise, then moved, sliding an inch higher, closer to her own face's height.

She stood a foot away, squinting against the darkness. Lucy thought of John, her time with him, how things had ended, and that gave her confidence.

"Who are you?" she asked.

"Help... me..." it said in a voice far more child-like than its appearance suggested.

Lucy marveled as its mouth moved, the dark outlines on the wall matching the workings of facial muscles even though its mouth seemed too small. Her heart cracked. She was glad she hadn't fled the house in terror.

"Yes, yes, I can help. You don't have to be afraid." She reached out a hand, placing her fingertips against the wall next to the face, offering comfort. "Whatever happened, whatever is happening, I can try to help."

"I'm... scared..." it said.

"I'm here. You don't need to be scared, okay? Just... tell me what's happening. Tell me what you need."

"Need... help... Lucy."

"You know my name?" Could this be someone she knew?

"Help," it said again.

Then it was gone.

"No, don't go," Lucy said. "I can help you. Come back. Please, come back and let me help you!"

Her phone rang, and Lucy jumped a mile.

"Jesus!" she shouted. The phone was in her purse, which she had set on the floor. Before grabbing it, she looked back at the wall, still empty. Lucy turned on the hall light and answered the call.

"H-hello?" She could hear the tremor in her own

voice.

"Hey, Lucy?" It was Meredith.

"Yeah, yeah."

"Whoa, are you okay? You sound kinda... I don't know. Panicked?"

"I'm fine."

"You don't sound fine, Lucy. You keep saying that to me, and soon it won't mean anything at all."

"Mer, I'm good. Okay?"

"Want me to come over? You seemed a bit off tonight."

"I did?"

"Well, I know we're both still going through a lot, but I got this vibe that there was something else on your mind. Something new, maybe. And now that I'm home, I'm a bit worried about you."

"Meredith, come on. I'm f—"

"Don't say it."

"—ine."

"You said it again."

"I did, yeah. And I mean it." Lucy looked at the wall again. It wasn't there, but she could still feel its eyes. Maybe having company wasn't the worst idea.

"Are you sure?" Meredith asked. "When someone is fine, they don't typically say it a hundred times."

"I'm sure. What about you?"

"What about me?"

"Are you okay? Do you want to come over?" Lucy asked.

"Maybe. Is that weird?"

"Of course it's not weird. I mean, we're both so fragile right now. Come on over for a nightcap."

It was a joke, and it made Meredith chuckle. They

were both recovering alcoholics.

"Alright," Meredith said. "I promise I won't stay long."

Lucy hung up, then tidied up the house, wiping counters and picking up a few things. She fed her cat, Eckley. He came bounding into the kitchen upon hearing the food hitting the metal bowl, like he always did. She adopted him just a few days after she met John, mainly because Eckley had started waiting on her porch each morning and partly because she needed something to take care of. He was a big cat with black fur that faded to a smoky gray in a few large areas. She wondered if he might have one of the bigger breeds mixed in. He didn't have the tufts of a Maine Coon, but maybe one of those big Norwegian kinds.

Meredith arrived, and Lucy made tea.

"You said something about a face?" Meredith said once they were seated on Lucy's couch.

"I did?"

"Right when we got to the restaurant, yeah. After that, you seemed more distant. I kept waiting for it to pass, but it was like you were preoccupied the whole rest of the night."

"I guess I was, yeah."

"You still seem like it, Lucy. I tried to tell myself to let it go, but I couldn't. And that comment about the face, well, it threw me. Will you please just tell me what's going on? We have to help each other."

That much was certainly true. They were codependent, propping each other up. Lucy was starting to think it was selfish to hold back and make Meredith worry about her when the poor woman had enough of her own worries to contend with.

"Yeah," Lucy said. "I'll tell you. But first, I have to say that it's not going to make a lot of sense. You'll think I'm nuts."

"Please," Meredith said, and that one word was enough to warm Lucy up, to make her comfortable sharing it.

"I've been seeing this... face. Like, in the shadows." She paused, expecting Meredith to interrupt with a question or objection. She didn't, bless her. "I don't really know what it is, or what it means. And of course, at first, I thought it was just... like an illusion. Or a projection or whatever. Just in my head. But right before you called, I realized it's not."

"It's not what? Not in your head?"

Lucy nodded. "It's there." She let that sit. "It talked to me. And I talked back."

"I don't... Lucy, I don't understand."

"I know. I don't expect you to, but I'm telling you anyway because I don't want you worrying about things I'm holding back. Weird as it sounds, you don't need to worry about me talking to it. Because it's... it just needs help. This could end up being a long night if I keep pulling you down this path, Mer, but... well, I'm... I guess you'd say I'm kinda..."

Meredith's eyes widened while Lucy struggled for the right word then decided there wasn't one. There was a list of incomplete words, but none of them were right. She chose instead one she hoped would be easier to understand, at least in its basic meaning. A word with a clear usage.

"I'm... I guess you'd call it psy—"

Before Lucy could finish, there was a loud banging

noise from the hallway, like something large hitting the wall.

"Did you hear that?" Meredith asked.

"Yes."

The noise came again, then repeated.

*BANG.*

*BANG.*

Lucy rose and walked toward the kitchen.

She flipped on the light and scanned the room, seeing everything in its place and nothing amiss. What could have caused that noise?

Suddenly, Meredith screamed.

Lucy ran back to the other room. Meredith was lying on her back, her spine arched, her chest pushed toward the ceiling and her body contorted to a painful-looking degree. Her mouth was open, but there was no sound. There was a shadowy, inhuman figure perched on her stomach reaching its dark limb into Meredith's mouth as if it had shoved a hand down her throat.

She turned her head toward Lucy, her eyes wide and pleading. The thing sitting atop her turned, too, and Lucy recognized its face. It had more depth to it than before but otherwise was a perfect match. She had seen it at the restaurant, and on her wall earlier. Had spoken to it.

It pulled itself free from Meredith and rose several inches off the floor, hovering and nebulous. Meredith's head dropped to the floor, and she was still. Her chest looked sunken, caved-in, her t-shirt folding on itself just below the collar.

"Stronger," the apparition said.

Lucy's mind stuttered, unable to process what she

was seeing and how quickly it happened. She had learned some degree of control over her psychic abilities throughout the last few months, but using them required strict concentration.

It floated toward her, a grimace stretching its horse-like features even further, opening its mouth large enough to fit Lucy's full head inside easily. A deep groan erupted from somewhere within it, impossibly, starting soft but building in volume the closer it got to her.

"No!" Lucy shouted, raising her arms in defense, protecting her own face in case it tried to reach inside her like it had poor Meredith. As her hands came up, it looked as if the vaporous creature ran into a wall and stopped. Instinctively, she pushed her palms closer to it, willing it to back up. When this actually caused it to move farther away, she was shocked, but quick-witted enough to take advantage. A look of surprise overtook its bizarre features.

Lucy felt a surge of adrenaline, which brought clarity. She closed both hands into fists and whipped them away from each other, picturing herself tearing thin cloth.

The black form of the entity—whatever this thing was that tricked her and then killed her friend—tore down its middle, a bright sliver of light escaping from inside it. Its groan became an abrupt screech, then the room was silent.

Lucy took a few quick breaths, then ran out the front door without looking back, wholly unsure of where she was going but knowing that whatever had just happened was only the beginning.

An hour later, unseen, the face reappeared in the shadowy hallway of her home.

It moved toward the nearest window, sliding silently along the wall like time-lapsed footage of spreading mold.

To be continued...

# The Fall of Allen Sutton

## Edmund Stone

The casket sat hovering over the opening of the grave. It looked like a foreign obelisk lying on its side, awaiting its cumbersome connection with the ground below. A large canvas canopy covered the grave site as a light mist of rain fell on the grounds outside the enclosure, cementing the feeling of desperation inhabiting the funeral proceedings.

Allen stood over the casket top, sniffing and clearing his throat. The box his dead wife lay in was closed and had been for the entire funeral. He was fine with it. The last thing he wanted to see was his beautiful Nicole in the state she was in when she died. He knew the mortician fixed things. The body he saw when asked to identify her wouldn't be the same as the one inside, but it was the one he would always see. His memory was forever etched with her mutilated face, the charred area around the bullet wound, the side of her head nearly disinte-grated. If suicide was her intention, she succeeded quite well. The only thing Allen couldn't piece together was why. Nicole's family, waiting outside the canopy, felt the same way, only their deduction of events meant Allen had something to do with it.

Allen had never seen eye to eye with Nicole's broth-ers. Jessie and Nathan McCarthy sized him up imme-diately when he and Nicole first dated. They didn't like him because he wasn't an athlete, wasn't a redneck like most in this area. Allen was a bit of an outsider if any-thing else, and they seemed to resent him for this. When Nicole's family, especially her brothers, found out about the suicide, their immediate suspicions fell upon Allen. They were grieving just as he was, but instead of seeing this for what it was, they wanted to place blame. He supposed he could see why he was an easy target. They had it out for him already. Nicole's brothers were the reason they left Salt Flat to begin with.

Nicole's family was very protective of her. She was the only girl, and her mamma was long dead, died in childbirth when Nicole was born. They had reasons to be protective, but Allen never gave them a reason to think he would harm her in any way. The opposite was true. He worshiped the ground Nicole stood on.

It made for a precarious situation. Allen tried to ex-plain to Jessie and Nathan he had nothing to do with this, but they weren't listening. His dad was the only one. Sy Sutton had a heart of gold and would be by his side even if they all deserted him.

Allen placed the bouquet he was holding on the cas-ket. His hands shook and his mouth quivered as he tried to say a few words. It came out in a whisper. "You didn't deserve this, Nicole. Why would you leave me? Why take our child with you?"

His eyes welled with moisture, and he sniffed as a tear rolled along his cheek. The minister over the proceedings began his prayer. Allen felt a hand on his shoulder as he bowed his head. The preacher's words trailed into a haze of swirling thoughts, mixing fervently through Allen's mind. He was somewhere else. A place of hurt and accusation. He wanted answers; he needed to know what happened to Nicole. He raised his head and straightened when he heard amen, then turned to see his dad looking at him with a somber expression. He spread his arms wide and brought Allen in for an embrace. His dad held him tightly, squeezing him with the strength of his days working in the mine.

"Thanks, Dad," Allen said, then felt the grip ease.

"I know this is hard for you, son. It's rough on all of us," Sy said. "But family will get you through."

Allen nodded. "You're right. But I have so many questions."

"I know, but give the police time and they'll figure this out. Right now, you have to heal. That's all that matters. Your health."

Sy started to speak again but was interrupted. "So, Sutton, now that my sister is done, what do you have to say for yourself?" Jesse McCarthy muttered, loud enough to cause those standing nearby to shuffle nervously. Jesse stepped toward Allen and pointed finger, ready to jab, like a joust through the heart.

Nathan grabbed his brother's arm and jumped in front of him, placing two hands on Jesse's chest, attempting to hold him back. "C'mon, Jesse, this ain't the place," he pleaded. Jesse outweighed him by at least fifty pounds, and Nathan's efforts, although valiant, weren't phasing the oncoming truck.

"Get out of my way, Nathan, Sutton has this coming," Jesse growled.

"Henry!" Sy called out. "Do something."

Henry McCarthy stood idly by, shaking his head at Sy.

Sy let out an exasperated sigh. "So that's how it's gonna be? Can't show at least a little respect for my boy? He's grieving just like the rest of us."

"I guarantee your boy ain't hurt like me. I lost my only daughter. That's like losing my wife again. If your boy had something to do with it, then retribution should be coming," Henry sneered.

Jesse pushed Nathan away, knocking his brother sideways. He bolted toward Allen, pushing him so quickly that Allen barely had time to react. He stumbled backward into the casket, striking it with his body. He fell unceremoniously on his ass near the opening of the grave, moving the turf sideways. His hand sunk into the fresh dirt underneath. The casket listed sideways, and the corner thudded against the ground, off the rails it had sat neatly on.

Allen, horrified at the sight, pulled his hand from the dirt and placed it on the box where his wife lay. His handprint smeared across the smooth, painted surface of the casket as he dragged it slowly away. He cried, then jumped when he felt a sharp pain in his side. Jesse's boot hit his ribs hard. Allen gasped, taking in a ragged breath.

"Jesse! Stop it. This ain't right." Allen heard Nathan pleading with his brother. As Allen prepared for the next barrage, he heard another voice, one dearer to his heart.

"That's enough!" Sy said.

Allen looked up at his dad. The man was older, but the younger, stouter version seemed to be appearing now. He had two hands on Jesse, looking up at the behemoth with eyes that could burn holes through steel.

Jesse pushed back though. "Out of my way, old man. I'll beat both of you to a pulp if I have to."

Allen wanted none of this. Tears streamed down his face as he looked at the casket, his handprint staring back at him. He propped himself on an elbow and watched while the melee ensued. His dad yelled at Henry McCarthy to do something and watched with disgust at Henry's continued indifference toward the situation.

Allen heard them, but as he tried to regain control of his body, he heard something else as well. A voice in the distance was calling to him. One he recognized. It sounded like Nicole. He looked at the casket, but it wasn't coming from there. It was farther away. Somewhere in the cemetery. He rose to his hands and knees and teetered there for a moment, then he stood and stumbled away from the canopy.

Sy and Jesse were still bickering. Henry and Nathan were in the mix now, pointing fingers and shoving. They seemed to forget what they were fighting about as they paid no attention to Allen.

He shuffled haphazardly forward onto the fresh-cut grass, feeling the coolness of the misting rain on his face. The ground gave under his weight, and he felt his foot sink into the wet earth. A low rumble shook through him, into his feet then up his legs and to the rest of his body. Some small part of him wanted to turn and run, but deep down he knew he should keep going to whatever was out there. It felt like an obsession. A calling to a higher power. Allen couldn't explain it but knew he must go.

Various tombstones lay scattered in front of him, the smaller among the larger, like steps to a temple leading to nowhere. Between them a fissure formed, working across the ground toward him in a ragged line. Steam rose from it slowly, listing like fog rolling on the ground. Allen could see forms coming from within the smoke screen. A hand crawled near the crack in the earth, flexing its fingers and grasping the dirt for purchase. It was gray and looked cold as it moved with no rhyme or reason, disjointed in its strange movements. Allen felt a chill down his spine as he waited for the body attached to the hand, but there was none. The hand was all alone, cut off at mid-forearm. A jagged piece of flesh hung where the rest of the arm should have been.

There was no blood. The thing looked dead, like something Allen had seen in an old zombie movie, and he hesitated before going farther. Then he noticed more movement in the mist. Other body parts appeared, hands, legs, and torsos, all writhing along the ground, moving to meet in front of Allen like a pile of snakes falling and rolling into one another. They seemed to have no purpose as they meandered along. The mist grew higher while it rolled along the grave markers, filling in the spaces until nothing could be seen. Even the body parts became covered.

Allen was confused. He looked behind him to where the canopy was located, but he couldn't see it anymore. It was covered with fog like everything else. He turned back and took a step, then stopped. Allen saw a girl ahead of him. It was his Nicole. She appeared as she was found in the house after her suicide. Half her head was gone. Only a hole where her eye should have been, a crater created by the bullet that killed her, and dried blood on the edge of the cavity, remained.

It made Allen cringe to see it. He stepped closer, shaking with fear at the horror before him. Maybe she wasn't there at all and this was a figment of his imagination. He wasn't sure, but knew he was being called to her for some reason, like a siren lures a boat to its unsuspecting death. But this was different; this was his wife calling him.

Allen felt the ground give again beneath his feet but paid no attention, only kept his eyes on her. He failed to notice the crack near his feet was spreading, getting larger, swallowing up the real estate around him. Something was reaching out, as well—large, snaking appendages, tentacles with snapping mouths adorning the bottoms. One grabbed his ankle, and he was stopped in his tracks.

Allen was immediately taken from his trance and concentrated on the things at his feet. They tugged and pulled, lacerating his skin. He screamed, reaching toward Nicole. But her image faded and another took its place. A woman stood there, beautiful, with dark hair and olive skin, like she was of Middle Eastern descent. Her body was covered with what looked like brands, but as Allen looked closer, he could see there were scars on her skin. The areas pulsed with energy, and he was instantly mesmerized as the longing for her increased. Blood oozed slowly from the marks on her body, dripping from her skin onto the ground, snaking from her in Allen's direction.

The tentacles had his feet and made it impossible to go anywhere. All he could do was watch her. The woman's head turned disjointedly, like something from another reality, not alive or dead but present in a realm the human eye shouldn't be able to see. Her head continued to tremble as she locked her gaze on Allen.

Her mouth opened, and she spoke to him with a voice coming from within his mind, echoing deep inside. He felt something grab his wrists and pull. Allen looked to see the dead hands holding him. He struggled, but they were too strong for him to pull away. Then he felt a tug at the back of his shirt and could feel something walk up his back. It was another hand, and he screamed as its cold fingers dug into his scalp and pulled his head backward in an uncomfortable position, forcing him to look at her.

The blood continued creeping toward Allen, covering his feet and easing up his legs to his knees, soaking his clothes. The hands that held him trembled with what seemed like anticipation. The blood rolled past his waist, and he could feel it inside his pants, stroking him as if trying to elicit an erection. Allen was surprised to see it worked. He was hard even though he had no immediate thoughts of sex. The opposite was true. But as the blood continued to move rhythmically in his pants, he found himself desiring the woman in front of him. She called, and he wanted to respond with everything in him. He knew it was a bad idea, that nothing good could come of this, but the desire remained anyway.

Allen was mesmerized by her and felt drunk with love for the woman. The tentacles eased and the hands pushed him toward her. The snaking appendages slithered into the ground and reemerged from the woman's side. The snapping mouths were still very present, biting the air in front of Allen's face. They wrapped around him and squeezed.

Allen screamed again, a fresh protest as the tentacles pulled at him, turning him to face the canopy where he was earlier. He saw his dad coming for him, yelling, but Allen couldn't hear him, only watched as his mouth moved. It was like a dream he couldn't wake from. The blood was now around his neck and continued to caress him lovingly, massaging his skin as it pulsed with life.

His dad was reaching for him now, nearly upon him. The ground trembled beneath him and the crack in the earth grew. Allen saw his dad's face as he stopped before Allen fell into the crack. He wore a worried expression as he tiptoed near the crack, reaching in vain for his son. Allen felt himself sinking into the ground. The tentacles and hands released him, allowing him to fall into whatever was below. It wasn't sudden, but a slow-motion descent. Allen looked down and saw nothing but darkness as pieces of dirt and rock fell, disappearing into the abyss below.

He fell faster, picking up speed as he looked at his dad and mouthed, *Help me*. But it was too late. Allen clawed at the air in front of him, desperately trying to grasp something. He heard his dad calling for him, but it faded as he tumbled out of control. He had thoughts in his head, memories of Nicole and the child she had been incubating to life.

But those thoughts were fading, replaced by the alluring desire for the one he saw in the cemetery, the one who's name came to him before he fell into deep slumber. Her name was Rebecca.

# PIECES PARTS

## JUDITH SONNET

She inherited this hyper-specific rage from her father. Whenever the family gathered together in the car, they all took a collective breath before hitting the road, knowing things would only be peaceful for a moment before someone cut them off, failed to use their turn signal, lingered too long at a stop sign, or drove a car that vexed him. Their father, a big and blustery man anyway, grew irate the second *anything* set him off when he was behind the wheel. And mom driving didn't fix things, either, because he was just as crabby in the passenger seat as he was in the driver's. Once, when he had actually rolled his window down to shout at an old lady who had been going ten below the speed limit, Carrie had crossed her heart and promised to never get as angry as her father did when she was old enough to drive.

But like most childhood promises, this was quickly broken and forgotten.

"C'mon, Carrie. Focus on the road," Platt muttered.

Ignoring her boyfriend, Carrie laid her palm flat on the horn and leaned in like it was going to run away from her.

"Bastard!" she shouted.

"Just ignore it, dear."

"Ignore it? How can I? He about *ran us off the road*!"

"He did not," Platt whined. "Please, you don't have to make such a—"

She rolled her window down. Before it was even halfway, she stuck her head out and screeched, "Learn to drive, fuckhead!"

The wind smeared her red hair around like blood beneath a finger pad. Her green eyes were slanted with anger, and her pale lips curled over her white teeth.

The car ahead of them picked up speed, as if it was trying to run away from her. She couldn't explain why, but this flushed her with contradicting feelings. Half of her was ecstatic she caused the opposing driver fear. Another half was aggrieved he would try and evade justice. She stepped on the gas briefly, causing the car to jump forward. Her father had called this "goosing." He said it whenever her mother chastised him.

"You're gonna get us in a wreck someday!" she would whine.

"Ah, I just goosed the car. Nothin' dangerous!" her father would chortled.

Carrie and her brother had both been terrified to eat in the car, worried their father would goose it and they would spill whatever food items they had on their laps onto the floor.

Feeling ashamed, knowing she was just like her old

man, who ironically died in an accident on a rainy night, Carrie looked over at her man. Platt was wringing his hands together. His curly brown hair even looked greased with nervous sweat. His beady eyes were shut tightly, and his brow was crinkled.

"Sorry," Carrie admitted before easing off the gas.

Ahead of them, the other car shot down the lane, weaving through traffic.

"He *is* driving like a maniac," Platt said.

Carrie snickered. "That's what I said."

"Still, it scares me when you get like this. I imagine the car turned upside down and our faces scraped off on the asphalt."

Carrie shuddered. She hadn't told Platt yet about her father. He knew the old man was dead, but not that his body had fallen out of the flipped car before it reached its final destination. Carrie saw blood streaked across the highway, clumps of skin and shards of shattered bone floating along the crimson trail like dead fish in a poisoned creek.

"You okay?" Platt asked, drawing Carrie out from her nightmares.

"Yes, I'm fine. Just... bugged."

"You don't bug easily. Until you're on the road, that is." Platt whistled and unclenched his hands. He spoke in a dainty, British accent.

Platt had moved to the States for work, and that was where they met. After only four months of dating, Carrie was confident Platt was going to ask her to marry him. She even convinced herself that the bulge in his pocket belonged to a jewelry case, concealing a diamond ring rather than a box of tic tacs.

Typically he drove, but they had gotten drunk and called an Uber last night, leaving his car at Deakin's Karaoke Bar, where they often met with their coworkers.

"At least we didn't make fools of ourselves last night," Platt said.

"That we know of."

"No. Anytime I get sloshed and make an ass out of myself, I wake up the next morning with a bad feeling about it. I may not know what I did or said, but I'll know I did or said *something*."

"You do a bad Cher impression." Carrie smirked.

"I'm as good a Cher as yer gonna get," Platt said.

They both laughed.

Carrie's happiness was cut short when a car stalled ahead of them. Despite having about thirty feet between them, she stomped on the brake as if her life depended on it. Platt fell forward, striking his head against the dashboard.

Carrie inched forward after the car ahead hit the gas. Leaning out the window, Carrie screamed at the driver, not even noticing her boyfriend. Platt leaned back, holding his head in his hands and groaning.

"Did you see that?" Carrie shouted. "Crazy fucking drivers, I swear! It's like the whole world has gone... *crazy*!" She released a flustered breath.

"Ugh, god..." Platt muttered.

Carrie turned and finally saw him. "What happened?" she asked meekly.

"*You* happened!" he snarled.

Carrie held her lips closed.

"Am I bleeding?" he asked.

"No."

"I'll get a lump, for sure."

"What happened?" Carrie repeated.

"You stomped on the brakes like a crazy person! I almost split my head!" Platt shouted.

"You saw it. That guy brake checked me—"

"No. He probably hit them by accident. You had plenty of time to come to a proper stop, but you went *nuts* instead."

Carrie shook her head. She knew it was her fault, but she wanted to defend herself anyway.

Platt looked as if he was about to say something more, but he stopped himself. Sighing, he lay back in his seat and rubbed his aching head.

"I'm sorry," Carrie said. "You know how I get when I drive. I'm on edge and—"

"Please, Carrie. My head hurts. Can't we just be quiet for a moment?"

"Okay, but—"

"Thank you."

"I just feel like I *need* to be on alert when—"

"Thank you, Carrie." He said it tersely, which caused Carrie's heart to break.

She studied the road, driving slowly and carefully, holding back her rage when other drivers made mistakes.

*I hope he gives me a chance to apologize*, Carrie thought. *I'd hate to leave things like this until work on Monday.*

"If there was a prescription for road rage, you'd be on it," her mother once told her father. Typically, he didn't respond to her jibs. For some reason, this stabbed him deeply. He made an effort on the next few that followed. But then, inevitably, he got cut off and the rage came foaming back.

*And I'm just like him*, Carrie thought. *I'll apologize, and Platt may forgive me... but then if another car pushes my buttons, I'll get right back to it—*

She carefully drove off the highway and toward Deakin's. Platt's car was in the lot where they left it. Carrie was thankful it appeared unmolested.

They sat in silence, Platt looking out the window, Carrie running her hands nervously over the ridges on the wheel.

"I love you, Carrie," Platt said.

"I love you too."

"I just don't love your *driving*."

She swallowed a lump. "I'm sorry. I mean that."

"I know you do. But we've had this conversation be-fore—"

"Have we?" Carrie was aghast.

"Twice now."

"I'm sorry. Really," Carrie repeated.

Another cloud of silence fell upon them.

Platt left without saying what she wanted to hear, which was, "It's alright. I forgive you."

Carrie tried to tell herself she was being silly for worry-ing so much, but she couldn't help herself. Whenever she closed her eyes, she saw Platt hitting his noggin on the dashboard—even though she had been too entrapped in her own anger to notice it when it happened, she could picture it clearly.

Sighing, she turned the wheel and drove down State Street once again. She had been going up and down the main strip on repeat, too worried to go back to her apartment and rest. Above her, the sky had grown cloudy. It would rain soon.

One second she was furious at Platt. If he was serious about their relationship, then shouldn't he have sat down and talked this through? But on the other hand. . . She recognized she was in the wrong and that if he was running away, it was because she pushed him.

She drove out of town and toward the country. Around her, hills rolled and sloped. The sky was crackling with thunder. It would be raining soon, and she needed to get home. If there was one thing she truly hated, it was driving in the rain—

She realized she was being tailgated.

Carrie shook her head. How had this gone unnoticed? Usually she was fast to catch someone messing with her on the road.

The headlights blurred her vision, obscuring any details of the car behind her.

She felt her fingers tighten around the wheel.

"Go around me, asshole," she muttered.

The headlights burned closer.

Carrie was about to throw her middle finger out the window when a sheet of rain hit the windshield. Gasping, she removed her hand from the button on the door that would have swept the window open and flooded the interior of her car.

*Christ, where'd all this rain spring from? It wasn't supposed to get* this *bad, was it?*

She grimaced, realizing she had thought this in Platt's gentle British voice.

*I wish we could have talked more. It's going to be so awkward at work on Monday—*

The car behind her nudged her, kissing her bumper with his.

Shocked, Carrie goosed her car. Underneath her, she could feel the tires spinning on the slick surface of the road.

Not caring anymore, she shook her fist toward the car and growled at it.

"You fucker! You tryna run me off the road? Huh? Huh?"

As if the driver could hear her.

She pressed on the gas. The other driver sped up, keeping his bumper against hers.

The rain was piling onto the windshield now, a thick glaze which buried her sight. But Carrie was too distracted by the driver to flick on her windshield wipers.

The car sped up, grinding itself against her. She sped up, desperate to escape her pursuer.

*This guy is fuckin' nuts!*

The car behind her honked its horn, bleating like a goat.

*That does it!*

She stomped on the brakes. Behind her, the car came speeding up! She couldn't believe it. Typically, the best way to get a nasty tailgater off your back was to brake check him. They didn't mind kissing your ass unless it resulted in a lawsuit! But this guy was *crazy!* She goosed the car again just before he hit her—

And then she hit the guardrail at full speed.

Without knowing it, she had driven right off the curve, which descended down a steep decline. She didn't quite believe she was crashing until her head connected with the roof of the car. She felt as if she had been put inside a washing machine and was tumbling about. She connected to the glass window beside her. She *felt* the window splinter. Then she was back on her butt, then she was lurching forward, the seatbelt pinching her. The airbag deployed, punching her like a boxer's glove.

Her teeth clacked together, spiderwebbing before they shattered.

All around her, she could hear the sounds of things breaking.

It was over as quickly as it had begun. The car was upside down. The airbag was deflated. Carrie hung suspended from her seatbelt. She wavered in the air, her left arm broken in three places, her legs burning sticks. She looked around lazily and glumly, her mouth tacky and bleeding, her eyes swollen and sore.

She heard something outside the car.

Footsteps.

The rain chinked against the undercarriage. She could hear water rushing down the incline after her.

"Help..." Carrie muttered. "Please, God..."

The door was torn away from its hinges and tossed behind the figure of a shadowy man.

Carrie blinked, too confuddled to realize that the man who had come down to see her had ripped the door off the car with his bare hands.

The man—the driver, she knew that—spoke in a guttural voice.

"This... is... all... I... *need*!"

He reached in and took her wrist. Unable to stop him or even argue with him, Carrie watched in stunned silence as he dragged her right hand toward him. Then he pried her index finger out of her fist. With a twist, he removed the finger. It came away easily, like the tab from a soda can. She screamed as her blood leaped away from the ragged stump and coated his grinning face.

She saw him then. . .

He was a composition of pieces and parts. Two different colored eyes sat on a face made of patchwork skin tones. His head was littered with different types and strands of hair. Long blond locks, grey tufts, brown curls, red rivers.

His clothes were a hodgepodge, mixing different fabrics and types together as if the original articles had grown holes which had been filled with pieces from totally clashing outfits. His getup looked clownish and would have been funny were it not for his ghastly face and the disturbing circumstances.

Even his hands were *jigsawed* together. The fingers belonged to different races, ages, and genders—

Except for the stump on his right hand where his index finger should have been.

Smiling, he showed her the finger he removed from her. It bled in his hand, flexing like a worm on a hook.

"I'll... be... complete... soon..." the cobbled-together man gurgled.

Carrie wailed helplessly.

The worst of it was she could still feel her index finger.

She could feel the rumpled texture of his fist as it closed over it.

She could feel the rain sliding through his hand as he walked up to his car.

She could feel it as it was inserted into his stump then sewed on with twine.

And years later, she would still feel it, lying against the bumpy ridges of the driver's wheel.

She would never stop feeling it—

# TALKING TAG

## JON COHN

"Get your hands off of me!" the Hollywood wannabe screams as two of my cousins drag him from the barn. I think his name is Pete. "Please! I won't tell anyone, just let me go!"

I hate it when they beg. Honestly, I think I just dislike yelling in general. Maybe if I had grown up hearing people shout things like, "Nice pitch, Jon!" instead of, "Oh god, oh god, please don't light my hair on fire," things might be different. Ah well, you play with the hand you're dealt.

If only the guy getting dragged across the lawn would get the memo, I could get back to my conversation with Carol from casting. Even if Pete were somehow miraculously going to escape the Krentler Media company picnic, it's not like he's ever going to make it as a leading man in this state. His eye is completely swollen shut and leaking a yellowish fluid that is *not* blood. The eyeball inside is probably done for. Also, it looks like he's missing a finger or two. I can't tell for sure, but I would make a solid wager he's missing some teeth. From what my brother, Todd, says, Pete auditioned for Krentler Media and was dumb enough to tell them he would run away from his family in Florida and told no one from his old life he was leaving. If only Pete could see the writing on the wall as clearly as the rest of us, maybe he would quiet down a bit and just let the party take its course.

Carol shakes her head, then takes a sip of wine. While she's only five-foot-two, she easily stands out as one of the most noticeable people at the party. She wears oversized turtle-rimmed glasses and totes a wild white hairdo that would make Andy Warhol jealous.

"You know, it's one thing if they die during our *Slashtag* playtests, but I have to admit it's kind of a shame when you get a winner and he still has to go. It would be nice if I could go back to having my casting talents result in hiring people that actually survive."

"What about Jeremy?" I say, pointing at the former film student trying to blend in. "He was a playtester, and now he's part of the Krentler family."

Carol snorts. "He's Lucy's pet. She says she let him live because he might be useful to production."

She leans over to me but doesn't quiet her words. "Also, you didn't hear this from me, but the real reason she had me cast him is because she wanted to boink him. I bet you a hundred dollars by the next company picnic he'll be a rotting skeleton in some basement."

"Jesus, Carol," I say with a snicker. "You're not supposed to talk like that anymore. We're in a post #metoo world."

"Ah, who gives a fuck. Look around, kid, these people have been doing what they're doing for three times longer than you've been alive. You really think any of them are going to mind their Ps and Qs now?"

I soak in the scenery around me. We're gathered at the Bartlett ranch, which sits between Los Angeles and the ghost town of Dire. Though to call this a ranch is kind of an understatement. It's more like a thirty-million-dollar compound, where dozens of construction and crew members for *Slashtag* have been living for the last year, renovating the old Propitius Hotel in Dire for the premiere.

I'm surrounded by some of the most successful people in America, all of whom are affiliated with Krentler Media in some way. While scanning the guests, I inadvertently make eye contact with my father, Charles Menuscha. He's in the center of a circle with some Hollywood royalty and acknowledges me with a blink-and-you'll-miss-it tightening of the lips. Not that the two of us would have much to talk about, anyway. It's been nearly six years since the two of us have spoken. Indirectly, my brother has acted as an intermediary, relaying the occasional demand or just to remind me of my father's general disappointment.

There's a noticeable shift in the atmosphere, and it's not because Pete's finally been shackled to a table and gagged over by the buffet. The guests of honor have emerged from the villa and cross the expansive grass field to join the party. It's William Krentler, the boss and founder of Krentler Media. His thin, spotted skin hangs off his skull like taffy, his eyes hide inside of a pair of twin purple caves, and his hair is nothing more than a whisper floating in the breeze.

Next to him strides his daughter, Lucy, in an expensive black dress with a red blazer that looks like pure confidence spun into fabric. Lucy has been working on an executive level of Krentler Media since she was twenty-one, but she has really taken the spotlight since spearheading *Slashtag*. Everyone laughed when she first said it, but they've come around to the idea she actually is the perfect person to also play as host for the biggest horror reality competition in the history of television.

Behind Lucy, intentionally disappearing in her shadow, is her brother, Billy, the spitting image of his father. Billy Krentler is only thirty-five, though by looking at the cracks in his face and his weary eyes you would think he's pushing fifty. Billy is the one who really runs Krentler Media since his father is in his nineties and his sister has dedicated all her time to running *Slashtag*.

Todd brings up the rear. His chestnut hair is shaggy and unkempt. Even though most of us are dressed casually, Todd is wearing a scuffed suit and a crooked tie, making him look messier than if he just put on a polo and khakis. From what he tells me about working for Lucy, I wouldn't be surprised if he has been stuck in that suit for the last three days. He's got Lucy's handbag hanging from his elbow, and he's frantically typing something onto a tablet as Lucy talks at him through the side of her mouth. I want to feel bad for the guy, but at least he's still in the business. If I hadn't shit the bed at the company picnic six years ago, I would probably be head writer on *Slashtag* by now. Instead, I'm lucky enough to keep a pity invite at the annual reunion thanks to my father being on the company's Board of Directors.

Carol knocks back the final third of her champagne glass, then hands it to me. "Sorry, kid, the uber boss is here. Always nice chatting, but you know how it is."

I nod. "If I were you, I wouldn't want to be seen with me either."

"You're a good kid," Carol says, patting me on the shoulder as she walks away. "That's your problem."

I consider trying to make my way into the awkward outskirts of a group's circle of conversation, but aside from rebels like Carol, most of the people here barely even tolerate me. Maybe if Pete would stop screaming into that gag, he and I could have a chat. I bet he would probably like a quiche and some champagne to cool the nerves.

Instead, I feel a pair of eyes lock onto me from the crowd. Like a shark, Lucy Krentler cuts through the crowd of bigwigs to me. Todd notices and hurries to follow.

"You're the one that brought disgrace to your family's name, right?"

"I also go by Jon," I say.

"Funny. You want back in or not, Menuscha?"

I nearly drop both glasses from my hands. I've been replaying my moment of shame for over half a decade now. Even though my own family won't talk to me, I know how lucky I am to even still be alive. People far more influential than me have been sent to the pits for much less.

"Can you even do that?" I ask, then watch as my brother's eyes go wide. Behind Lucy, he shakes his head emphatically like I just shoved my foot into my mouth.

"I'm Lucy Fucking Krentler, I can do anything I want."

"Sorry," I say, now stumbling over myself to correct my attitude. "I just sort of meant, why? No offense, but there's more wealth and global power on this property right now than the rest of the world combined. What the heck do you want with me?"

"Everyone here is either old money or has their face plastered across billboards in Times Square. I need someone who's believable as a younger, pampered, rich asshole. Better than everyone else but hasn't actually done anything to earn it. Can you pull that off?"

"I think so?" I say, feeling a cocktail of opportunity and humiliation.

Lucy draws a circle around my face with her finger. "That stupid look you have on your face right now? Don't change a thing." And just like that, Lucy turns to find her next target. "Todd, fill him in on the rest. I've only been looking at Jon's face for a minute and I already want to punch it. He's perfect."

Todd casts me a nervous smile as Lucy stalks off. "Sorry to ambush you like that. She's not what most people would call, um, nice. Please don't tell her I said that."

I finish my drink, then drop both glasses next to a tree. "Who am I going to tell? I'm practically excommunicated. You're the one on the fast track to being the next director of whatever."

Todd shrugs. "I don't know. I don't think she likes me very much. This job isn't really as awesome as it seems."

"No shit." I can't help but laugh.

He laughs too, finally letting some of that nervous energy out. "It's good to see you." He wraps his arms around me.

"You, too," I reply, squeezing him back.

"And it's not all just verbal abuse and a hundred-hour work week. I do have some perks, like I get to eat in the executive lunchroom instead of the regular one."

"And it sounds like you were able to get some sort of job for me?" I ask, redirecting him back to the matter at hand.

"Oh, yeah! If it works out, you'll be fully back in the family, which would really be great. Dad could go back to insulting both of us instead of saving it all up for me."

"Can't wait." I'm trying to keep cool, imagining the heights I could reach if I got back into Krentler and company's good graces and balancing that with whatever fundamental part of myself I would have to compromise in order to get there. "So what do I do?"

Todd shrugs. "I guess she needs someone to pretend to be a douchey CEO of a new health juice company and convince some YouTuber to be their spokesperson."

"Why doesn't she have you do it?" I ask.

Todd glances down at his shoes. "She said I'm about as douchey as a donkey. I'm not even sure what that means, but I don't think it's good."

"And if I do this, I'm just back? What does that even mean, exactly?"

Todd nods, perking up. "You'll have your monthly deposits resumed, Dad promises to stop ignoring you, and I got you a podcast."

"A podcast?" I ask.

"Well, they're not just going to suddenly have you writing movies. But it'll be, like, it's own whole website, slashtaginsider.com, and you can have the podcast going simultaneously as *Slashtag* is airing. If you do a good job with that, maybe you'll get picked up to do the novelization of the show or something."

"And all I have to do is this one thing?"

I feel the weight of his next words loom heavily. I know what he's going to say. Ever since Lucy first mentioned the opportunity, I've known the catch.

Todd bobs his head from side to side, reluctant to say it. "You know, you have to do 'the thing.' It's not that bad, I promise. Even I was able to do it, right?"

For six years, I've had to live with the shame of passing what was meant for me over to my brother. Today, he's passing it back to me. There is no negotiation here. After this I'm either moving into a McMansion in Calabasas or heading home to four roommates sharing one bathroom in Los Feliz.

"Fine. I'll do it."

Fifteen minutes later, Lucy is giving a lavish speech for her father, ninety percent of which is about herself. I barely even hear it; my ears tingle and my lips go numb. In my hand is the heavy steel hilt of an old blade. Beside me lies Pete. I wish I'd given him a quiche earlier.

There's a round of applause, and I tune back in to Lucy's speech.

"To honor our host, let's all enjoy a good old-fashioned sacrifice!"

The crowd roars with excitement as Lucy gestures to me.

"And to thank Charles Menuscha for his generous contributions to *Slashtag*, here's his son, Jon, back for a second try!"

I watch the faces that have shown me nothing but coldness and disdain for half a decade now cheering for me. Some, like my father, still hold looks of trepidation, surely wondering if I'll squander this second chance as well.

Pete is screaming something, but I can't make out the words through the mask. His shirt has been ripped open, his hands and legs tied to the corners of the table. Though one eye is gone, the other one stares at me, pleading for mercy, just like that other girl last time.

Why do they always have to look at me? Whenever I give blood, I always look away from the needle. Who wants to watch their own execution? And again, Pete, why all the screaming? What's that going to do for you right now other than make me annoyed enough to want to kill you even more? It's not endearing.

My hand starts to shake. An eighty-five-year-old governor who probably can't even figure out how to right-click on a computer somehow has his phone on video mode so he doesn't miss a second. Several others follow in his wake—the president of that shoe company, the guy who owns the music business, they're all record-ing me.

Petey screams again, this time loud enough it makes my ear twitch into my shoulder.

That's it. I hate yelling. I raise the knife over my head, then bring it down as hard as I can into his chest until I feel the blade's tip dig into the wooden table beneath him. He screeches so loudly that I climb up onto the picnic bench and yank the knife out, only to drive it in again and again. Splatters of blood slurp out of him every time my knife rips from his wounds. Distantly, I can hear a crowd going wild. Cheers and laughter egg me on, replacing Pete's dying screams as I drive the knife repeatedly into his chest until I'm able to reach in and rip out a piece of the mangled heart inside. I hold it over my head, squeezing it like a sponge as I drain its juice onto my already blood-soaked face. My mouth tastes like iron, and some of Pete's blood runs up my nostril and tickles my sinuses, causing me to do a combination of a sneeze and cough that nearly results in me vomiting. A sudden wave of reality takes over, and a piece of me comes back to my senses after this obscene frenzy.

But then I look out at the crowd and see nothing but pure elation. The Krentlers, my brother, even my father are looking at me with beaming pride.

I just killed a man for a penthouse and a podcast. And it was worth it.

# Morskegul

## Andrew Najberg

Overhead, pale-green fluorescent tubes hang under their hoods from the dilapidated parking garage ceiling, buzzing erratically like a hornet trapped behind blinds. Many have blinked out altogether, and their lack of illumination only seems to highlight the shadows of the gouged cement pillars, the roof collapsing in chunks. The air smells of strong bleach and even stronger of something rotten. It has long been said most animals seek a quiet place to suffer. No doubt a dog or coyote crawled under one of the parked jeeps and died. Probably of some cancer. Or blood poisoning. Or parasites. I took a walk one evening last week and saw a stray cat from whose bloated belly writhing worms actively fell while she prowled.

My heel bumps against my black duffel as I shift to rub the aching spot under my ribs. The lumps beneath the skin that chafe between the bones have edges. Hard things shift in the sinew. I feel like things are being cut inside me, and my insides churn. The doctors who examined it after I showed it at my annual pronounced it benign, but the cyst has ballooned in the last few hours. I think about that cat and half expect something to burrow through the skin and come wriggling out to the ground.

It's worth it, I tell myself. It's worth it for Liska. To get her out of that gulag.

From the concrete shore walk beyond the ocean wall, moans and hums rise from the sea organ, the instrument that plays the tides like whalesong, the melody the locals call Morskegul. It digs into your bones like fingers grasping from a world forgotten, a world where there were whales in the ocean, where people wondered what music the waves would make if they swept into a giant instrument.

Placing a cigarillo between my teeth, I rap my lighter's base on the edge of the crate upon which I sit before I strike flint and drag. The garage around me is cold and still and so full of echoes that even the sizzle of my ember echoes around me. The tobacco is old-grown from sealed emergency stores and tastes faintly of rubbing alcohol and ammonia. The burn in my lungs makes my forehead sweat, but the nicotine still makes my fingers buzz and my head light in an instant.

"Those things'll kill you," people used to say about them. And I say, "Fantastic."

I turn my lighter over in my palm. It's long tarnished, but the engraving, "To G, Love L," is still legible, from my sometimes-sweet sister in a world where there is so little room for loyalty to blood. The metal of the lighter is cool as I press the lid against my forehead and close my eyes. I try to bring her face into my mind, but all I can see is the black hood they slid over her head the day they marched her out of our home.

"Lucky we don't take you too," the Sergeant in beige uniform had said.

I didn't say it, but I disagreed then, just as I do now. Better the gulag than to serve the Bureau with a disgraced name. At least one can climb the social order in the prison; The Bureau will grind the dishonored down under their bootheel every chance they get.

I nod to myself, look at my hand under the orange glow of the cigarillo's cherry. I had smoked them fresh from the black market before Liska was taken. Of course, I was complicit even if she chose to confess that I was not. Our identities are all just accumulations of the little greeds that reflect angles inside us.

Just then, footsteps clop from somewhere down the aisle. Stubbing the smoke with a twinge of regret that I had just barely started, I slither to my feet, my legs oddly wobbly, the words, "You're late," about to grate from my lips. My side aches. It throws me further off-kilter, so I press my palm against the cyst as if I'm trying to hold an organ inside a gaping wound.

Before I see the origin of the footsteps, I spot down the aisle two shadows stretching toward me. Krieskov is not alone. That he and his companion entered in silence is no good sign. I reach into my cargo pocket with my free hand and close my fist around one end of an oblong leather pouch filled with iron beads. It's no hole puncher, but it'll do in a pinch if I get close enough.

I step close to the side of a personnel truck. The tattered canvas hood over the bed smells of sweat and shit. In the uneven light, I spot through a hole in the cover that blood residue streaks the bed. The smell of bleach is much stronger where I stand. No doubt they unloaded the dead and wounded and then poured chemicals onto the metal flooring. Perhaps someone inside had been writhing with the slow pumps of desperation, not knowing that for all purposes they were dead already.

The dead never quite know they are dead. Only that death comes.

I glance back to where I left my duffel. I can't quite see it in the shadow of the crate where I had waited.

The steps reach the edge of the truck, and I step out.

Krieskov's eyes widen like moons under his bushy eyebrows, and his mouth opens in a silent gasp, revealing those shattered front teeth and canines. As he tells it, when his rank was fourth secretariat he had been cornered by thugs who hoped his satchel held saleable documents; they had struck his upper lip with a hammer. Now they are jagged, brown and yellow, caked with tar and plaque.

The man with him steps back, drops his hand to his belt. He's broad shouldered and bald as a fender. His hand closes on a pistol as I raise my blackjack. He thinks what I think, no doubt: will the barrel raise before my beads drop?

"Hey," Krieskov says, stepping back, raising both hands up, palms out. "We all take deep breath, yes? If we kill each other at hello, the only one who wins are Bureau accountants who pocket our last paychecks."

The bald man's upper lip twitches.

I raise my free hand back to the throbbing spot of

my ribs. The shirt is wet. The wetness is sticky. I lower my weapon slowly so my sleeve conceals the glistening bulge.

"Besides, is this any way for you to greet an old colleague?" Krieskov says.

"Been a long time since we jockeyed desks together, Krieskov," I say. "And The Bureau's scraping my assignments from underneath the barrel now because they think the bottom too good."

"Ach," Krieskov exclaims like he's clearing his throat. "What good do we gain from grousing over what function The Bureau thinks we should play? We should be thankful we have a function at all."

I nod, glance at my watch.

"You're late," I say.

"Bratzo was late," Krieskov says, tipping his head toward his companion.

"Bratzo shouldn't be here at all."

"Ah, friend," Bratzo says, flashing a folded paper bearing The Bureau's seal. "It's the Bureau that says I should be here."

He holds the paper into the light. Official orders for sure, but I don't read the particulars. Why trouble whether they dotted all the Is on what I assume will turn out in the fine print to be my death warrant? No matter, really. The outcome of our dialogue will be the same either way.

"Then here you shall be," I say, gesturing my free hand to the garage around us. "After all, as they say, it's the third hand that fills out the paperwork."

We all chuckle, but Bratzo's hand doesn't leave his gun. He wears grey slacks and a green administrative shirt with the name "Rayka" stitched over the breast pocket, but I see the scars that edge out from under his collar. The tattoo on his neck in the shape of a pierced star. Figures they would send a specialist. I can practically smell the things he has killed with those stocky hands. Is that blood under his fingernails? I should have cracked his skull open the second I stepped out from behind the truck.

Krieskov brushes dirt or crumbs off his shoulders. He removes a flask from his inner pocket and takes a sip. He does not offer me any.

"Enough of these pleasantries," Krieskov says. He reaches out and places a hand on the outside of my bicep. On the other side of the bicep, I feel the blood pulse through the cyst. If only Krieskov knew how close his hand is to something he does not want to touch. Then he continues. "You bear word from the Gollitok?"

I tilt my ear and listen to the sea organ like it brings me a new message. It's like the wind into a cave except it teases like something orderly will come. Like there is sense to be made. The notes rise and fall, a vibration that throbs in my knuckles.

"Better," I say. I gesture vaguely to where I had been sitting, though they do not know where I had been sitting nor that I left a duffel there. "A sample has been retrieved."

Both Krieskov and Bratzo exchange a glance.

"The Cekic Compound?" Krieskov says, his voice pinched.

I nod.

"Confirmed?" Bratzo says, raising his eyebrows.

I flex my bicep. Underneath it, the hard nodules in the

cyst grind against each other, silent. Unseen, a shudder runs through them, and I become aware of a webbing path that runs from my ribs down to the seat of my belly, down my thigh and calf. Right to the line where the seawater among the rocks lapped my ankle when I stepped forward to retrieve the motorized buoy. Somewhere beneath that is where the drops of the sample spattered. The whole foot below is a cold and brittle thing inside my shoe. Even at that first moment, I knew something truly grave had transpired.

"Confirmed," I say.

Krieskov draws a deep breath.

"I see," he says.

His eyes drop to my hands. One hand is empty other than the sticky, clear slime that coats it, which I doubt he can see, and the other still holds the blackjack, which hangs impotently.

He looks to Bratzo. Looks down to the hand on Bratzo's pistol. "This changes things."

Bratzo rolls his shoulders.

"Does it?"

Krieskov frowns.

Something in my ribs grinds. Like shattered glass. I wince.

"What's the matter with him?" Bratzo asks.

Krieskov turns to me, takes a step back. His brows knit.

"There is much in this world that disagrees with me," I say, bringing my sticky hand to my belly. "And today, the first among them is my lunch."

Bratzo narrows his eyes at me, pokes me in the chest and leaves his index finger pressing a dimple into my shirt breast.

"Eating off the black market, no doubt," he says. "Like all the other pigs on the fringe."

I smile snidely. Take my hand from my stomach. Reach up. The movement to me is slowed down. Like the air thickened around me. My hand closes over his firmly. I pull it down and toss it to the side.

His arm swings back as his pistol comes clean from his belt, and he thrusts the revolver toward me. The barrel stops almost in the exact spot where his finger had just been. I can't keep my eyes off his hand, though. I can almost see a stain on his skin where I touched him.

I smirk on one side of my mouth until Kierskov barks, "Enough of this."

Spittle flies from his lips between myself and Bratzo. Bratzo's gaze is frozen cobalt. No muscles in his face move. As if time stopped within his soul.

The dead never quite know they are dead. Sometimes they don't know that death comes.

Krieskov places his hand on the barrel of the revolver and slides it down. I hear that knuckle crack of the hammer returning to its rest.

"Where is the sample?" Krieskov says.

I cock my head toward the crate.

"In the duffel," I say.

Krieskov smacks Bratzo on the shoulder. Bratzo scowls, though its unclear if it is at me or being struck, then he strides toward the crate. I watch his hand darken into the shadows around him as he steps farther out of the light.

Then Krieskov looks to me.

"What news on the team? Have they determined

Yost's objective?"

"Negative," I say. "The lieutenant is playing it close to the chest. Apparently, there is some antipathy between her and the lead."

"Varka? They have history?"

"Or she is just being Yost," I say. "No doubt she is unwilling to trust the forward team so early into the survey."

I chuckle, and the vibration in my ribs sends lightning bolts of pain through my cyst. It shoots all over my body the way an exposed tooth nerve sends lances of pain through the skull. I supposed the cyst was just easiest to infest. It is my greatest vulnerability, other than Liska. I cringe.

"You don't look so good, comrade," Krieskov says. "Perhaps you should return to an orthodox diet. With the black market, it's too easy—"

"What is the meaning of this?" Bratzo calls from over by the crates. He is kneeling over something. An open box. Krieskov reaches inside his jacket and pulls out a high-watt penlight, clicks the beam on, and shines it on his companion and the box.

In the open box rests the shards of a broken glass capsule.

Krieskov mutters something under his breath. Takes a step back from Bratzo. Looks at me. Takes a step back from me too.

"What am I looking at?" Krieskov says.

My grin spreads wide from cheek to cheek even as the grinding and scraping of things inside me sends fresh agony from head to toe.

"Where did you plan to leave my body?" I ask through

grit teeth.

"My friend," Krieskov says. "How long have we known each other?"

"Enough to know that you'd accept the right price for my neck."

A hurt look spreads across Krieskov's face. It is not the hurt that he has been wrongfully accused. It is the hurt of distaste for an assignment he has also accepted. Every bureauman knows that look. It is usually followed by wiping bits of skull off your cheeks.

He pulls a pistol of his own and levels the barrel at my chest. Bratzo rises from the crate and takes aim as well.

I sigh.

"Is Liska still going to get the money?"

Weights drag Krieskov's face down. He takes a couple more steps back.

"You know this has gone well out the realm of things that get entered into ledgers," he says. "Have you been in contact with the compound?"

I hold up my palm. I know it still glistens in his penlight. I point to the wetness of my shirt.

Bratzo lowers the hand I touched from his gun and stares at it.

"What's really going on out there?" I ask.

"On the Gollitok? In the territories?" Krieskov asks, continuing his steady back pedal, casting suspicious glances to Bratzo now too. "Same as always—we are trying to take it back."

"Maybe we shouldn't have burned it down in the first place."

Krieskov shrugs. "It is what is," he says. "Maybe it is best for you then that I'm taking you out of it."

I hold up one finger, reach to the bottom of my shirt.

"Slowly," Krieskov says, stopping. Planting his feet with a little wiggle of the toes of his boot against the grit of the dirty cement.

Around us, the sea organ moans, throaty, deep. Its echo amplifies as if the world caught part of it and us in a jar. The lights are brighter than they had been, and the shadows swim with sparkling particles. I can see every single edge, including edges that aren't there, fractal patterns stretching off corners and angles. I want to step toward Krieskov, but my feet won't move.

I laugh softly as my shirt clears where the growth swells. It's no longer just a soft lump like part of an orange under my skin. The skin itself is brittle, flecked with wet, soppy crystals. It's almost scaly in a radiating pattern away from the central spot. On the lump itself, the crystal nodules look like the amethyst inside a geode burst through my skin, except that its spongy everywhere but the sharp edges. A syrupy fluid oozes down my skin.

"Is t-t-that—" Krieskov sputters.

"The sample?" I ask.

On impulse, I reach to the growth with my hand and close my palm over the pulsating lump. Instantly, I feel the edges sheer straight through my skin like a knife into gelatin. Something in the lump anchors into my palm, and as I draw my wrist back, the mass squelches loose in a clump. Thick threads of crystal-laden sinew and muscle slide out from my ribs like pumpkin innards. Like jellyfish tentacles. Longer and longer. The ropey slop glistens and drips with a foul-smelling ooze, streaked slightly with blood as if my own fluids had been mostly replaced by it. Chunks of bone slide out effortlessly with it, too, and dangle at odd angles–that must be a pair of my ribs grown to the twisting, flexible crystals. There goes a chunk of something deeper, part of my pelvis maybe?

I try to take another step, but the inside of my leg degloves from inside my skin, my foot having sluiced through my shoe and burrowed into the ground. The broken shaft of my tibia and fibula jut into the air from my immobile shoe as the rest of me pitches forward. It's strange; it doesn't hurt to have left part of myself behind. Rather–it's as if I can still feel it. Not like a phantom limb, though. Like the leg standing there is still a part of me. I can feel the soft breeze in the garage blowing over the bone shards, the pulsating muscle.

Krieskov's pistol roars, and a hole blasts in my chest. I feel each part of myself spray out, each bone fragment. Each chunk of meat. I can feel the fluid that filled the tendons that had been attached to my scapula sinking into cracks in the concrete. It's like I am the pavement too as I spread, as everything I touch becomes a bit of me.

I realize, too, that I feel myself in Bratzo's palm. That is me pressed against his other hand, steadying the pistol and its aim. He pulls the trigger and sprays more of me against the personnel transport.

"Don't shoot–you'll spread the infection," Krieskov orders, but Bratzo keeps firing.

I try to laugh, but my lungs are too perforated to hold air anymore. My cells divide all over everything. Consume. Absorb.

This isn't what I expected, but as Krieskov put it: it is

what is.

Despite the distance between us now as my old colleague continues to retreat, I can see that the tiniest drops of my blood have sprayed onto his clothes. His face. If I focus, I have the slightest awareness that I am there too.

He should, of course, call in a containment strike, have this whole garage annihilated in fire. But he is no different than any other compatriot. Only serves The Bureau to a fault when it fills his pockets too. It's a different matter to empty one's lungs for it.

Bratzo's weapon runs dry. It is when the flashes stop from his muzzle that I see his cheeks and the tears on them. He watches Krieskov turn and run and then reloads his own pistol.

He chambers a round, presses the muzzle to his temple, and fires. His body collapses instantly as his brains blast out from his skull. I am still all over his skin, and somehow, the instant he dies, it becomes easier to spread into his cells. Into the ground beneath his cells.

I regard his remains with curiosity. I wouldn't have expected him to do the correct thing. To have truly understood his part in the machine. If only Krieskov had been so noble.

For my part, I feel like a new machine firing up. It strikes me that I don't quite know what I am any more—but that I can see myself soon being everything there is. My awareness rises and falls on the music of Morskegul, the whalesong sea organ that people with dreams of a beautiful world once built against the waters. They once thought they could harness the endless force of ocean and current, the lap of waves and spray of brine and froth, into something to be enjoyed. I wonder if Liska will learn of my death or if they've already killed her too. I like to think that perhaps she sleeps, her head on a bundled cloth on the gulag floor, and that she dreams of the melody of the tides.

# THE MONA LISA EFFECT

## NICK BOTIC

On the side of a desolate road that traverses the equally desolate landscape of a region in the northern United States sits a nondescript structure. Its appearance is that of a warehouse one might spot among many similar buildings in the industrial district of any given city—gray brick marred by age and the elements, windows along the top third of the sides and the bottom third of the face, a flat roof. It is a place more often driven past than driven to as no signs advertise its existence, one of the innumerable, unremarkable edifices that adorn the sides of the winding avenues that make up the country's vascular system.

But for some, the building's out-of-place visage beckons. And when the building casts out its call, a driver might feel compelled to veer off the road and onto the dirt path that leads up to the building's front doors, which are perhaps the most distinct (if out of place) feature of the structure's exterior. The doors are made of ornate African Blackwood, with intricate designs hand-carved into them, spirals and cylindrical ravines both thin and wide, big and small. The knobs are similarly ostentatious, constructed of polished silver that glints in the country sunlight.

As a guest enters the building, they aren't met with a stand at which they might expect to purchase a ticket. Rather, there is no fee for admission, though even if there were, there would be no employee to conduct the transaction. This roadside museum is free and open to all travelers who find themselves coasting down the quiet avenue beside which it stands.

And as this curious visitor passes through the sumptuous entranceway, the effect will be staggering. For as plain and barren as the land surrounding the building is, and indeed the exterior of the building itself, the interior is a lesson in overindulgence, in garishness, in decadence. It appears as if the space within is several times larger than the outside would suggest, its cathedral ceilings far taller than the roof outside should allow, the walls untold feet more spaced apart. Hanging from the ceilings are three large crystal chandeliers lit by warm, jaundiced bulbs from within, shards of light bouncing about the walls. Below them is a large open-floor layout that is home to what should immediately inform any guests as to the nature of the building.

Statues and busts are featured prominently, cordoned by velvet ropes and lit from below by vivid white light. Hanging about the walls are scores of paintings from artists both modern and of eras past, in styles ranging

from photoreal to abstract to expressionist and everything between and beyond. The subjects of these myr-
iad works are invariably serene. They depict individu-
als who wear expressions of contentment across their
faces, landscapes composed of warm, peaceful beauty,
and families in a state that, while perhaps not reflective
of the time in which they or people like them may have
actually lived, appear to exhibit genuine happiness. Elderly men play chess in vibrant parks lush with autumn
foliage, renaissance women of privilege galavant about
uncharacteristically clean and maintained towns, children from some indefinite epoch frolic in the water of
an ocean as blue as sapphire and painted with such an
adept hand as to give the impression that if one were
to place a hand upon it, they would withdraw that hand
and find it damp and dripping with saltwater.

And at each end of the strange building's easternmost
wall are the entrance and exit of the Special Installation,
what could perhaps be considered this odd museum's
main attraction, in such a case that it did any attracting at
all. A sign hangs above the entryway as identification and
invites guests in, warning them, in spite of the darkness
beyond, to watch their step until they are afforded more
visibility.

When the guest steps past the threshold from the
main floor and into this special exhibit, the disorienting
effect of the museum's inner dimensions will be joined
by another similarly off-putting result—the space ahead,
which appears to be simple emptiness, will appear pos-
itively cavernous. The guest might wonder how this
building, as large as it may be in earnest, could possibly
contain such a vast amount of empty space. It is here

the guest may begin to feel their anxiety rise as their mind tries to make sense of the inconsistencies with this bizarre roadside museum. That anxiety, however, will be put at ease when a light bursts to life up ahead, and another to the right of the first, and a third to the right of the second. Each illuminated area is rectangular, each wider than it is tall, giving the impression of bay windows installed in the shallow face of this study in darkness. These windows and the light within them have their own unsettling feature—the light does not cast itself outward, leaving the area between it and the guest a river of absence. At that same time, the guest may realize the Special Installation's entrance, the one through which they just walked only moments ago, is now gone, replaced by an abject darkness of a purity identical to that which lay ahead.

The guest may then walk ahead, moving through the soupy black using the peculiarly lit windows ahead as its north star. As they reach the angle at which they can see through the glass, they will lay eyes upon this nameless museum's Special Installation.

Wax sculptures of people stand motionless behind the glass. The guest will marvel at the lifelike qualities of the sculptures, forgiving the places in which the fact they are indeed built of wax are made apparent. The eyes, after all, are the most difficult thing to recreate in any medium. What will truly captivate the guest, however, is what they will interpret as the installation's use of mirrors to convey the illusion of space. The wax people will appear to number in the hundreds, or even thousands, standing in a wholly disorganized fashion stretching back farther than the human eye is capable of seeing. The background against which they stand has been painted so as to depict an unfamiliar landscape, the ground a cracked mess of red clay, strange, monolithic towers in the distance, a dizzying collection of black stars resting about the cosmos above. The method of design which this canvas bears will imbue the guest with the illusion of motion, inviting them to fix their gaze upon any given area and see in their periphery the swirling void in which a thousand, thousand worlds exist and cease to exist in the span of a lingering glance.

The guest will almost certainly then become aware of the direction in which each and every one of those innumerable wax sculptures' eyes are so intensely focused, that direction being wherever the guest happens to be standing at any given moment, in an unsettling manipulation of the viewer's disorientation that might inspire questions of the artist's intent, as if this manufactured sensation of being watched was a curious byproduct of the exhibit's creation or a conscious decision meant to instill dread into the hapless passerby. Upon this realization, an audio recording will begin, one that explains the strange optical illusion known as the "Mona Lisa Effect," in which the eyes in a painting or other work of art follow the viewer around the room. Right around the part of the recording that informs the guest of a misnomer in nomenclature—that despite being named for Leonardo da Vinci's seminal work, the Mona Lisa doesn't actually exhibit the illusion—the guest may suddenly feel the need to question whether that wax sculpture's head, the one a row or two back from the glass, was turned at that angle when they last looked at it. And as they ponder that, they will begin wondering if all their heads were in the same positions they were a moment ago, and then if the bodies had changed position, too, and hadn't the space closest to the glass seemed less crowded?

The guest will likely assume there appears to be too many to have gotten a reliable idea of their positions, and by this time, the exit of the installation has opened! The yellow light from the main floor is pouring in at the opposite end of the hall, the same distance away from the windows as the entrance. The recording will finish up, and the guest will head back to the main showroom. But if the guest decides to look back before they exit the Special Installation area, they might see the wax sculptures all pushed against the windows, their faces twisted into violent, odious scowls, expressions with a malevolence as pure as the darkness to which they will return when their spotlights shut back off. Accompanying this fearsome display is a soundtrack that is only heard should the wax sculptures be looked upon, a soundtrack of tortured screams played in reverse and at a volume so low as to make the guest question if they're hearing it at all.

But whether their curiosity compelled them to take one last glance back at the wax sculptures or not, the guest will emerge from the Special Installation into a showroom with a decidedly different atmosphere than it had just minutes prior.

The paintings that once depicted joyous families now feature father raping daughter, mother smothering infant son, brother cannibalizing sister. Tranquil scenery has given way to sinister hellscapes, lands of smoke and ash littered with the brutalized cadavers of their unfortunate denizens. The expressions of statues and busts have transformed from happy or, at the least, optimistically indifferent to the same scornful grimaces as the wax figures. And some of the works, be they the horrors in paint or the horrors in clay, depict things not of this earth at all, writhing tentacular masses, hideous grotesqueries composed of innumerable limbs and eyes and mouths and possessing a fearsome apathy regarding the viewer and all of their kind.

And in each piece, in every medium, the eyes will seem to follow the guest as they make their hurried, petrified way to the museum's exit, the scores of gazes feeling almost physical in their weight, as though the figures casting them are piled atop the shoulders of the guests, slowing their pace and quickening their already rapidly-beating heart to the point of a cardiac episode.

And as the guest pushes back through those African Blackwood doors, they might hazard a look over their shoulder, where they will find among the hateful artwork scores of the wax figures with their baleful, lifelike gazes all leering with their scorned visages at the departing visitor. The guest will then leave the nameless museum, perhaps glancing in their rearview mirror, perhaps wondering if the building had been at such an angle before, this angle that makes it seem as if the front of the building is perfectly in line with them, its windows like eyes, windows that appear to be more numerous than they were when the guest approached the building.

The guest will go about their life, for a time, with the unmistakable feeling of having narrowly escaped a great and horrific danger. A week, perhaps a month, even a year or more may pass, but in due time, the Mona Lisa Effect and the consequences it wreaks on those unfortunate travelers who happened upon that outwardly, nondescript structure that houses that nameless museum will return. First it will be instances the guest can easily brush off as a result of their paranoid mind, a single magazine cover or a single person in a photograph of many. But before long, the guest will find the actors in every shot in a film or television show seem to be breaking the fourth wall for the sole purpose of peering directly at them, and even worse, all their eyes will have that same little something *off* about them, that minor incongruence characteristic of the wax sculptures in the Special Installation of that nameless museum. Soon the malignant, waxen eyes of every still photo, of every magazine cover and interior, every billboard, every advertisement, every animal both wild and domesticated, follow the guest. And by the end, every person—the guest's family and friends, coworkers, strangers—their eyes will follow. The guest may try to run, to escape the oppressive observance of any and all eyes, be they live or manufactured, but even if they manage to isolate themselves from the world and all its eyes, no respite will come. Their mind will make eyes where none are—from shapes and angles and even their own miodesopsias.

The eyes will never cease to follow them.

And the madness that accompanies being constantly watched will prove too much for the guest to handle.

And their last thought before making their most final decision will be of the recording in the Special Installation of that nameless museum on the side of that desolate road.

Of how the Mona Lisa doesn't even exhibit the properties of the effect that bears its name.

# Origin of The Species

## LM Kaplin

2000 BC - Luxor, Egypt
(1000 years before the events of *Fang Fiction*)

Aria covered her mouth with a linen cloth before entering the makeshift infirmary. Even after spending countless hours inside, she never grew accustomed to the putrid smell of rot and decay that filled the room. The wafting odor drifted with the wind throughout the encampment, but the diluted aroma in the air paled in comparison to the stench within the small building. The thin cloth covering her face did little to stem the awful smell, but at least it concealed the faces she made as she attempted not to gag on the odor while tending to the sick.

Looking at the sheer number of patients that filled the room, she felt an impending sense of failure. With many dying each day, and even more contracting the disease, caring for the ill had overwhelmed her. Although she had assistants who helped treat the afflicted, as high priestess, any blame for the lack of success in curing the victims fell squarely on her shoulders.

With so many people vying for her attention, she didn't know where to begin. Aria grew more disheartened with each passing day as the suffering of her people only increased. What began as red lesions on their skin turned into large boils that transmitted the illness through the air as they burst. She could easily spend all day cleaning the bloody puss that coated their blackened skin and still not make any headway in stemming the spread. Most of her assistants had fallen ill themselves, and it had become difficult to find new volunteers for the job. The villagers saw the fate of their peers and knew the job was a death sentence. It was a miracle Aria hadn't contracted the disease herself, but she knew her luck wouldn't last forever. She credited her good health on the protection of her goddess, Sekhmet.

As high priestess of the temple, it was her duty to fulfill the goddess's needs, and in return, Sekhmet offered prosperity to her people. Although Aria always performed each offering in accordance with Sekhmet's demands, the disease afflicting her people continued unabated. Aria didn't understand why their goddess had forsaken them.

As Aria surveyed the room, to her dismay she noticed more of her kin had perished during the night. Removing their bodies to make room for more patients was the top priority. The discolored corpses served only as a reminder to their neighbors of the fate they had in store.

She called on the men of her tribe to assist in the removal of the bodies, but even the bravest of warriors refused, fearing an enemy they could not see. Reluctantly, she dragged the dead, one by one, out to the burn pit on her own until the task was complete.

After disposing of the corpses and filling the beds with new patients, she returned her attention to the others. Knowing many were beyond the point of saving, slipping in and out of consciousness and barely aware of their surroundings, she was forced to decide between providing them comfort in their final hours or attempting to heal the newly infected before the disease ravaged their bodies, as well.

Aria knew the situation was dire. She ordered her last remaining assistant to grind up more of the healing paste used to treat the lesions. The combination of aloe, myrrh, and opium massaged into the open sores had failed to stop the infection, but she hoped it provided a respite from their pain.

After the mixture had been applied in generous amounts, there was little else she could do for them but pray. Aria returned to the temple's inner sanctum to plead with their goddess for an end to their agony.

Kneeling before the shrine, she took a moment to collect her thoughts in silence before beginning her prayer for help.

"O mighty Sekhmet, protector of the Pharaohs, goddess of war, and deity of healing, we are in need of your assistance. As you know, a great plague has spread across our land and killed many of our people. Even more are sick and will surely perish without your help. We are desperate for your powers of healing. I have adhered to your demands and followed your teachings to the best of my ability. If you care about our people, then answer our plea. I do not make this request lightly, for I fear we will all soon perish, leaving no one to guard your temple and provide the offerings you require."

The priestess waited for a response, knowing in her heart the goddess would not forsake her people in their time of need. As high priestess of the temple, Aria ensured she fulfilled the constant offerings of blood Sekhmet required. Having seen the goddess of war in action, Aria knew how important it was to keep Sekhmet's bloodlust at bay. But as she listened for a reply, the inner chamber remained silent.

Having exhausted all known remedies, and with the disease still ravaging her people, Sekhmet was their last hope. If the goddess failed to appear, her people would be no more.

After sacrificing countless of her kin over the years to retain the goddess's favor, for the first time in her life, Aria questioned if the blood she spilled for her deity had been for naught. Why did they sacrifice so many if Sekhmet did not protect them in their time of need as she had promised so many years ago?

Her clan had called on Sekhmet's blessing only once before. Aria was just a child at the time, but she still remembered the moment vividly. Her mother held the title of high priestess and allowed Aria to join her in the ceremonies, knowing that one day she would pass the sacred duties to her daughter. With their land under attack from the Nubians in the south, her mother entered the sacred temple to ask for the goddess's aid in war.

Based on her studies, Aria expected Sekhmet's help

to come in the form of increased strength and stamina for their warriors. So her mother seemed as surprised as she when a rumbling came from deep within the ground. The quake intensified, shaking the very floor they stood on. Aria clutched her mother's waist for balance, wondering if the temple would swallow them into the ground. When the disturbance subsided, a fissure had opened in the rock and they heard movement from within.

Aria and her mother stepped backward, clutching each other as a shadow swept across the walls. Before they took a second step in retreat, the goddess emerged from her tomb.

As Sekhmet came into view, Aria and her mother stood in awe of the deity's radiance. Although images of Sekhmet's form adorned statues and hieroglyphics throughout the village, the crude images did no justice to the majestic creature in front of them. Standing straight like a human, she had a slender waist with thin but muscular arms and legs. A golden coat of fur that shimmered in the candlelight covered the entirety of her body. Many thought the visage depicted in the drawings to be a mask or avatar, but Aria knew instantly the goddess displayed her true face. Sekmhet's features matched that of a giant feline, her snout adorned with large white whiskers. For the first time, Aria realized Sekhmet was more than just an invisible god who required blind faith in her authority. When Sekhmet spoke, the priestess and her daughter listened.

"Tell me, priestess," said the lioness. "What is so important that you have disturbed me from my slumber?"

Aria's mother stepped forward, doing her best to conceal the fear that seeped from every pore in her body.

"Dearest Sekhmet, protector of the Pharaohs, goddess of war, and deity of healing. Our city is under siege by an overwhelming army. We require your help in fending off the attackers and saving our people."

Aria still remembered the goddess's reply as if it were yesterday. The lioness's voice reverberated through the tomb, changing pitch as it echoed like a tuning fork. "It is true I can offer protection for your people, but my assistance comes at a cost. A cost that you may not be willing to bear."

Aria's mother replied, "O great one, I would not ask if we were not desperate. You are our only chance of survival against our enemies. Lend us your sword. We will pay the price you require."

"Then it is agreed. I will vanquish your enemies, but the cost must be paid in the blood of your own."

Without another word, Sekhmet emerged from the tomb, her first step outside the stone enclosure in over a hundred years. She looked up at the heavens, shielding her eyes from the harsh rays of the sun, and wondered if she would ever return to her home in the stars. She had reluctantly made this planet her home, and although Earth had its benefits, the yellow sun made her weak and burned her skin. She could not remember the last time she had felt its rays on her face and had forgotten the feel of its burn. The searing light stung, but her powers of healing and thick coat of fur protected the great feline from its light.

In a flash, the creature was gone, leaving Aria and her mother to ponder the fate of their people and wonder if the cost would be worth the goddess's protection.

Knowing that fleeing from their homeland was the only other option, the proud people refused to leave and hoped trusting in Sekhmet was the correct decision.

Word traveled quickly from village to village about the lion-faced heroine that fought on behalf of the Egyptians. By the time rumors of the great feline warrior reached the Nubians, they dismissed the stories as tall tales by a weakened enemy desperate to save themselves at any cost.

Unafraid of the legendary lioness, the Nubian army marched along the Nile towards Thebes, the capital of Upper Egypt. But when remnants of the first wave of soldiers returned to their camp speaking of a great massacre, King Kaa hardly believed their tales. Facing little resistance until that point as his great army marched through the villages of Egypt, he ordered his troops to push forward once again.

This time the Nubians advanced with the full might of their forces, yet they were still no match against the goddess. Sekhmet slaughtered the soldiers with ease, slashing their throats, ripping open their torsos and devouring their innards. With the ferocity of a lion and the immortality of a god, the slaughter left her with a lust for blood that could not be contained until every soldier had been torn limb from limb.

With the trespassers defeated, Sekhmet's taste for blood remained, and in her rage, she turned on her own people, devouring anyone who crossed her path. It was only when the high priestess, Aria's mother, stepped forward reciting an invocation as she approached that the goddess paused her carnage.

When Sekmhet's fury subsided, she spoke. "High

priestess of Luxor. Your request is complete. I have destroyed your enemies and saved your people. However, in doing so, I have awakened an ancient bloodlust inside of me that cannot be quelled. Now it is your turn to repay the favor. I will return to my tomb, where upon each full moon, you will deliver to me one of your own to satiate my appetite. As long as this oblation is met, your enemies will not dare encroach upon your land, for they will know you are under my protection. Fail to deliver what I require and I shall turn my wrath upon you once again."

Without another word, the lioness was gone as if she vanished into thin air, leaving Aria and her mother to interpret her words and rebuild their civilization.

Upon returning to their homes, the high priestess attempted to explain their new responsibility to her people, but after hearing the strange demand, the citizens of Luxor thought the priestess had lost her mind. Even after witnessing the goddess's power of destruction with their own eyes, they refused to believe in Sekhmet's curse.

With the villagers unwilling to abide by the goddess's demand, the priestess refused to condemn an unwilling candidate to death. Having no other choice, on the next full moon she entered the chamber and gave herself to the goddess. Hoping for a respite from the goddess, she found none and was devoured in front of her people. With her mother's sacrifice, Aria became the new hemet-netjer, servant of god, at a very young age.

After witnessing the great lioness slaughter the high priestess, the people's attitude quickly changed. Even the skeptics of the tribe instantly feared her and were humbled by her power. Since that day, a seemingly endless supply of volunteers were sent to the tomb to appease Sekhmet's need for blood. Each of the tributes died with honor, knowing they would be rewarded for their sacrifice in the afterlife.

Since then, the villagers lived in peace for years, and their civilization flourished under Sekhmet's protection. That was until recently, when the unseen foe entered their village—the plague that now devastated their people. So here was Aria, almost the same age as her mother when she called upon the goddess, knowing that any cure Sekhmet offered would again come at a price.

Standing inside the temple in the very spot where her mother pleaded for help all those years ago, Aria's resolve wavered. With only silence greeting her in return, she wondered if the goddess even heard her appeal.

Just as her hope for a reply dwindled, the temple rumbled to life as it did when she was a girl, and Sekhmet emerged once more. The goddess hadn't aged since their last encounter, emitting an aura of resplendence as she entered the chamber.

When Sekhmet spoke, her deep voice shook Aria to her core. "Bring them here. The sick. There is but one remedy for their illness. A taste of my blood is the cure they need. The life force within me will heal their ailments and grant them immortality."

Aria couldn't believe her ears. "Immortality?"

"It is not the boon you may think. In many ways, you will be immortal as I am, but unlike me, your bodies are frail. Where I am from, my species had millennia to adapt to our habitat. We grew thick coats that protected us from the cosmic radiation, but your sun is young and burns bright. We can withstand the harmful rays, but not forever. You, however, are not so lucky. With no time to acclimate to your new nature, you will be forced to dwell in the shadows for eternity, feeding on the very thing you once were."

Blinded by the prospect of immortality, Aria's decision had already been made. Standing before Sekhmet, she watched as the lioness used her claw to make an incision along her wrist. A black liquid seeped from the wound, oozing down her fur and dropping to the ground. The dirt sizzled as more of the tar-like substance pooled on the dusty stone floor. With the bloody arm held out to the priestess, Aria stepped forward and knelt before the goddess. Taking the slender extremity in her hands as if cradling a baby, she leaned forward to give it a kiss.

She pressed Sekhmet's arm to her lips as if hypnotized by the black gift dripping from the wound. She barely noticed the sour taste as she swallowed the first gulp of her deity's essence. One by one, Aria led each of her people down to the goddess's chamber, and one by one, they emerged from the tomb as something new, something different.

# Publisher's Note

Thank you for reading our Books of Horror Indie Brawl companion anthology. This competition and anthology wouldn't exist without you, the reader. We appreciate your continued support.

If you enjoyed this book, please consider leaving a review on Amazon, GoodReads, or your favorite social media platform.

Broken Brain Books is an indie publisher dedicated to helping authors share their stories with readers around the world. Please visit our website for more information about our releases and signed copies of our books. www.brokenbrainbooks.com

## Other Anthologies by Broken Brain Books
Screams From The Ocean Floor
Screams From Beyond The Veil

## Also available
Rorschach by Aaron Lebold
Mine by LM Kaplin
Fang Fiction by LM Kaplin
Ruby's Cube by Lyla Diamond

# About the Authors

## Gage Greenwood

Gage Greenwood is the best-selling author of the Winter's Myths Saga, and Bunker Dogs. He's a proud member of the Horror Writers Association and Science Fiction and Fantasy Writers association. He's been an actor, comedian, podcaster, and even the Vice President of an escape room company. Since childhood, he's been a big fan of comic books, horror movies, and depressing music that fills him with existential dread. Find out more, at www.gagegreenwood.com

## John Durgin

John Durgin is a proud active HWA member and life-long horror fan. Growing up in New Hampshire, he discovered Stephen King much younger than most probably should have, reading IT before he reached high school—and knew from that moment on he wanted to write horror. He had his first story accepted in the summer of 2021 in the Beach Bodies anthology through DarkLit Press. His debut novel, The Cursed Among Us was released June 3, 2022, and went on to become an Amazon bestseller. Next up, his sophomore novel titled Inside The Devil's Nest, released in January of 2023, followed by his debut collection, Sleeping In The Fire in June of 2023. In 2024 he is set to release two more novels, starting with Kosa, and Consumed by Evil through Crystal Lake Publishing in the fall.
Website- www.johndurginauthor.com

Twitter- @jdurgin1084 | TikTok- @johndurgin_author | Instagram- @durginpencildrawings

## Angel Van Atta

Angel Van Atta writes horror as a way to spread the same kind of hope that she so needed as a little girl and outside of the world of fiction only really ever found as an adult. The kind of hope that tells you that good often overcomes evil and that anything is possible if you just believe. Her stories are vivid and chilling as well as heartwarming and fast paced. She invites you to walk with her in her imagination. A place that can be just as dark as it is light.

## Mike Salt

Mike Salt was born once... But then immediately raised by wolves. He spent the majority of his childhood fighting to survive in the forest. Cold. Alone. Mike learned English by snatching various paperbacks from campsites and off hikers. He is feral. He is in need of a bath. Don't trust him. But read his work. It's fine.
It's fine.

## Jay Bower

Jay Bower is a horror author living outside St. Louis, MO in the forest of southern Illinois. He spends his time reading, writing, and convincing his wife the dark stories he writes do not involve her. He's the author of The Dark Sacrifice, the Dead Blood Series, and Hanging Corpses. Find out more and sign-up for his newsletter (and receive a FREE story) at jaybowerauthor.com.

## Leigh Kenny

Leigh was born and raised in the garden county of Wicklow, Ireland. She lives by the Irish Sea with the love of her life and their two wonderful boys. Her debut, Cursed, released in December 2023. Her next book is coming soon. You can find out more about Leigh's work on her social media pages at Leigh Kenny Writes.

## Debra Castaneda

Debra Castaneda is an award-winning horror and dark fiction author based on the central coast of California. Her works include *The Spore Queen*, *A Dark and Rising Tide*, *The Root Witch*, and other titles in the Dark Earth Rising series of standalone novels.

Debra loves writing character-driven stories about people who experience scary things, and how they react when confronted with the unexpected. She's committed to representing Latinas and Latinos in her books. For inspiration, she draws from her experience as a TV and radio journalist, and as a third-generation Mexican American.

## Devin Cabrera

Devin Cabrera, a former filmmaker turned author, brings a cinematic edge to his gripping novels. With "Welcome to Nightmare Island" and "Jones 1963," he ventures into the realms of suspense and horror, captivating readers with his vivid storytelling. Drawing from his experience in the film industry, Cabrera infuses his narratives with immersive scenes and dynamic characters. Through his transition to literature, he continues to showcase his talent for crafting compelling stories that linger in the imagination. Devin lives in upstate New York. When he's not writing, you can find him hiking through the mountains, exploring caves, and trying to find the perfect slice of pizza.

## DE McCluskey

D E McCluskey was born in 1973, in Liverpool, England. He is the author of novels, graphic novels and comics. He lives with his daughter (an author in her own right (at the age of 8) with her children's adventure The Hangry Hamster), his partner, her daughter, and a sausage dog called Ted.

## Justin Boote

Justin Boote is an English author living in Barcelona and has been writing horrorfiction for approx. 8 years. In this time he has published around 15 novels and three short story collections. He also writes extreme horror under J.Boote which he does not necessarily recommend you read if you're squeamish!

You can find all of his books on Amazon and KU under Justin Boote and J.Boote(extreme horror pen name).

## Caitlin Marceau

Caitlin Marceau is a queer Canadian author and illustrator known for her award-winning novella *This Is Where We Talk Things Out*. Her forthcoming work includes her debut novel, *It Wasn't Supposed To Go Like This*, and her second novella, *I'm Having Regrets*. For more, find her on social media or check out CaitlinMarceau.ca.

## Jeff Strand

Jeff Strand is the Bram Stoker Award-winning author of sixty books, including PRESSURE, DWELLER, and THE ODDS. He does not condone brawling and wishes this was the Books of Horror Indie Loving Embrace. You can visit his Gleefully Macabre website at www.JeffStrand.com.

## Ben Young

Ben lives in the Cincinnati, OH area with his family and dogs, where he is currently working on more stories which may or may not ever see the light of day. He does not enjoy writing about himself, especially in the third person like this. Find him online at www.benyoungstories.com

## Edmund Stone

Edmund Stone is a horror writer and part time boat captain living on the Ohio River. But mostly he lives in his head where he derives a wealth of characters and strange ideas. He's even seen a few strange things crawling from the water. He lives with his wife, four dogs, and a plethora of cats.

## Judith Sonnet

JUDITH SONNET is a very sad girl. She writes gross and disturbing horror books, and she collects old paperbacks as well as 70's action movies. She grew up in Missouri, but now she lives in Utah. She's trans, asexual, and is an abuse and suicide survivor. If you want to know more about her, check her out on Facebook... or contact her through your nearest Ouija board. She is the author of Beast of Burden, Summer Never Ends, Low Blasphemy, and No One Rides For Free. She has curated two anthologies, SCRAPS and GASPS.

## Jon Cohn

Jon Cohn is a horror novelist and professional board game designer based out of San Diego. He's written books like *The Island Mother, Slashtag, Try Not To Die on Slashtag* and *Everything Is Temporary*. Jon is very excited to finally be able to merge horror books and games together by bringing *Ghostland* to life as a board game. For other upcoming horror games, keep an eye out for *Basket Case,* and *Black Christmas* coming later this year, along with *Thanksgiving*, which Jon co-designed with Eli Roth himself!

For autographed books, head to www.joncohnauthor.com, or sign up for his newsletter for free short stories and games! You can stay caught up with him at @joncohnauthor on Facebook, Instagram and TikTok.

## Andrew Najberg

Andrew Najberg is the author of the best-selling (#1 US Horror Amazon) novels *The Mobius Door* (Wicked House Publishing, 2023) and *Golli-tok* (Wicked House Publishing, 2023), as well as *The Neverborn Thief* (Olive-Ridley Press, 2024), the forthcoming collection of short fiction *In Those Fading Stars* (Crystal Lake Publishing, 2024) and the forthcoming novel *Extinction Dream* (Wicked House Publishing,

2025). His short fiction has appeared in *Fusion Fragment, Khoreo, Translunar Travelers Lounge, Utopia Science Fiction, Prose Online, Psychopomp Review, Solar Press Horror Anthology,* and is forthcoming in *Make Your Presence Known* Anthology, and the *Gods and Globes III* Anthology. Currently, he teaches for the University of Tennessee at Chattanooga.

## Nick Botic

Nick has been writing since 2016, and has seen his work featured in various anthologies, magazines, and podcasts. His debut novel Daughter's Drawings released in July 2023 to overwhelmingly positive reviews. He currently lives in the Milwaukee area with his fiancée, Kimmy, and their five cats.

## LM Kaplin

LM Kaplin is an author from upstate New York who has been a horror enthusiast in all forms his entire life. His morbid obsession with the macabre began one night while watching Poltergeist as a young child. The next morning, he began searching for ancient burial grounds in the backyard. Dismayed at not uncovering any evil spirits, he buried his own demons for future generations to find. It's time to start digging them up. He is the author of "Mine" and "Fang Fiction."